A Tale of The Feyra
Tale 4

Dee

And The Golden Cartouche

George R. Mead

E-Cat Worlds Press

Dee and The Golden Cartouche

LCCN 2013935471

Mead, George R.
Dee and The People /
George R. Mead.
p. cm. – Dee and The Golden Cartouche (A Tale Of The Feyra; Tale 4)
ISBN-13 978-0-9890927-0-8
1. Fantasy. I. Title. II. Series.

E-Cat Worlds established its publishing program as a reaction to the large commercial publishing houses currently dominating the book industry and the smaller intellectual clones. It is interested in publishing works of fiction and non-fiction that are often deemed insufficiently profitable or commercial or that are not necessarily reflective of current literary trends and fads.

E-Cat Worlds, 57744 Foothill Road, La Grande OR 97850
www.ecatworldspress.com
SAN 255-6383

In the middle of nowhere - Creativity.

First Edition:
Printed in the United States of America

From Grandeville.

Portal
Lair
Search
Not Again
And Again.
Magiwitch
Rebirth
Offspring
Holiday
Treasure
E'Nilt
Braidna

A Tale of The Feyra

Jonathon and Dee
Dee Of The Fontala
Dee and The People
Dee and The Golden Cartouche

Nonfiction

A History of Union County
The Ethnobotany of the California Indians
A History of The Chinese in The West: 1848-1880
Yachats. The Town Called "Dark Water at the Foot of the Mountains."

Stirrings

New Mexico.

The gentle breeze drifted lazy softness across the desert and tickled a piece of sand here and a piece of sand there. It poked soft fingers at the flowers of Spring which barely nodded.

Unseen and unfelt, the almost not there wind filtered over and around and through the town of Santa Fe, sitting in the clear sunlight bright and clean, sitting there for four hundred years or so, at 7,260 feet above sea level.

They were gathered in a large room, in the home of their founder, to discuss the information that each of them had gathered during the past year as well as to share that which members who could not attend had sent in.

The interior of the room was painted in soft yellow tones with a rather elaborate design painted on the ceiling. This design was an amalgam of various local Native American designs. The building was one of the older abode structures in town dating very far back in the town's history.

All of the members, present, or not present, wore a gold band on some finger on their right hand. These rings had a slightly raised round emblem of a blazing sun delicately etched into them. The great windows were open wide. The window sills and surrounding walls were thick, reflecting the earliest construction techniques utilizing dry clay blocks. The soft breeze drifted soft caress inside to gentle touch around the group gathered there. They hardly felt it.

The most senior member called them to order and began the discussion of whatever had been learned since the last annual meeting.

The group was comprised of the membership of a small and dedicated group seeking the origins of the vampire and werewolf mythologies which they all believed was a reflection, however altered by the passage of time and the wandering of folklore from reality to myth, of a real group of beings although no-one, not anyone in their group, believed in shape shifting. They believed that the interaction of this group's behavior with the rest of humanity in antiquity had given rise to the development of the various mythologies which occurred mostly in Medieval and later times as the Christian church sought to cast non-believers into becoming creatures of evil and darkness. It was that past that they were most interested in. They believed it would explain much of what they felt was a lost history.

The meeting wandered on into the night and finally, as it always did, consensus was reached. It was decided that the group would now focus their research in the more isolated and mountainous regions of Europe. It seemed to them that most of the mythology had developed in such settings.

One of their members told them that he was developing a different lead and that it would, for some time, take him in a different direction. All agreed. It was up to each of them to follow that which they felt was most appropriate.

They stood, raised their glasses, and saluted the portrait of their founder, and dispersed to carry on his and their work.

Daniel Fanzle, the one following a different direction, had always had a very high level of curiosity about everything. This had carried him in directions that others rarely followed. He was very glad that he had left his previous employment and had started his own enterprise. What he did now was ever more interesting and never boring.

It was his habit to always arrive a few days prior to the meeting and drift from art gallery to art gallery around the immediate area. Santa Fe had many such places. Sometimes he bought a piece of art that appealed to him, but mostly he just looked. It was a relaxing activity and it gave him time to ponder whatever his curiosity had been attracted to.

Not all members of their small group could make the annual meeting due to the cost and their economic standing. He had no problem in either aspect. But other than his habit of always paying cash for everything, there was no sign of his economic standing. He didn't wear expensive, tailored anything. His dress was always rather casual and bought in rather inexpensive shops. It was just a preference, a habit, of a sort, from his student days, more that than anything else. If a shop or business asked for identification he offered them his driver's license. The face was his, the name was not, nor was the address, nor any of the other information on it. But it would all stand up to most scrutiny that anyone wished to make. He was a very private person and wished to remain so.

At their annual meeting no-one wore name tags nor were introductions made, one to the other. All conversation was focused on their mutual interest and nothing else. The gist of the meeting was written down and the pages left in selected spots, visited now and then by those who couldn't attend. They were all rather private persons, as much as they could be.

Now, mid-morning of the next day, Daniel was once again drifting from art gallery to art gallery. He was puzzling over a stray bit of information that he had read. His staff had seen it and had made sure that he received it. Perhaps this was just the usual over-blown nonsense that passed as reporting these days, perhaps not. But his curiosity had been caught by it.

He hadn't shared this bit at the meeting. And he wouldn't until he felt that it was really something that ought to be shared. He had found that much of what was shared was, to his way of thinking, less than reliable.

So, he visited this art shop and that art gallery, a very quiet and unobtrusive visitor.

He was quiet because he felt like it. It was his choice.

He was unobtrusive because of his physique and his facial features, factors which made him one of the people that were seen but never remembered. It was his genetics.

So, as he wandered from shop to shop he pondered the few bits and pieces that he had recently gathered and came to a decision. It was time to go and talk with some folk and see what else he might learn.

He had always enjoyed talking with people whenever he was in the mood for that type of activity. It was one of his long ago surprises that people enjoyed talking with him.

It had dawned on him quite some time ago. He always remembered that time.

He had been visiting one of the large cities on the west coast finishing up a piece of business, one of the results of his curiosity. In this case it had turned into a very profitable piece of business. It didn't always happen. But this time it had.

That evening he had enjoyed a play, one of Shakespeare's longer stories, then he had a long, late, and casual dinner, and after that had taken a walk, just to stroll about the area, just to mull over some new thing that he was pondering.

He wound up standing in front of a rather antique looking small diner that was still open in the wee hours of the morning, around 3:00 a.m. or so.

In front of the place next to the street there was a small stall selling newspapers and some magazines. The owner was a rather battered looking man of indeterminate age.

Daniel had asked him about the food inside the establishment and about the business of selling newspapers and magazines in this location and so on and so forth.

They had moved inside the place, sat on stools at the counter, and ate chilli and drank coffee, which Daniel had ordered for both of them, continued their conversation, and had been joined by two others who knew the stall owner and were equally battered looking. Soon the four of them were engaged in a wandering conversation about a large number of topics.

Then it had happened.

A man had walked in and sat on Daniel's free side. Much to Daniel's surprise this stranger then told him that he did not like him, not even a little bit. Daniel told him that was all right and began to talk with the others again. But the man continued to interrupt and stated with greater vigor how he didn't like Daniel.

The two on the other side of the stall owner stood, stepped around, and said, ever so politely, that it was time for this stranger to vacate the premises. Now!

He looked at them, at their very worn out clothes and weatherbeaten faces, their facial expressions, got up and left. The man behind the counter smiled at the four and refilled all the coffee cups.

The group finally wound up their conversations as the sun began to rise into the dawn. The group dispersed but only after Daniel was patted on an arm or shoulder.

Outside on the sidewalk, the stall owner said, "Nice talking to you." He closed and locked the stall and started down the street. He paused, turned, and waved jauntily. "See ya." Then he headed into a side street.

Daniel never forgot.

Washington, D.C.

He strolled down the hallway, dressed in the standard dark blue suit of the political elite, very expensive, neatly tailored with matching light blue shirt, and a red tie. He passed offices that were mostly quiet in this early part of the evening. Now and then he waved and smiled at the few hard workers that were finishing up in order to be ready for the next morning's burst of activity and meetings that were the normal part of doing business here in the center of the nation's government.

As he turned through the main intersection toward his offices, a man passed him going in the opposite direction.

The man smiled at him in passing. "Evening, Tim." And headed for the outer door.

Timothy Grimble hesitated for a few steps and then started walking again, brows furrowing in thought, if not worry.

What was he doing here? He chewed his lip. Only that one person could stroll so nonchalantly down this hall, stroll so casually from the President's Office, at any time of the day or night.

Then he shrugged and opened the door to his office suite, his private domain. Everything was proceeding according to his plan, little by little, inch by inch, with nothing leaking to the beasts of the media.

His secretary, always there until he left for the day, handed him a stack of messages and a filled cup of coffee. She seemed to have her own network and always knew when he was headed for this office.

He closed the door to his office, sat in his chair behind the desk, took a sip from his cup, set it on the desk, and began to thumb through the messages and finally found the one that he was expecting.

He read it, dropped it into the paper shredder, and smiled. Right on schedule. He almost laughed out loud.

It didn't really matter what the President discussed with that guy, the one that he had inherited from the previous President, in some strange way only known by the past and present President.

Things were going exactly as he had planned. He smiled.

Northern Maine.

The remains were in the middle of a very large clearing at the end of a narrow road. Heavy forest surrounded the clearing and both sides of the narrow road. The road started about a mile from the edge of the nearby small town and ended here. All the wreckage was inside some sort of log palisade.

Daniel had strolled from debris pile to debris pile and finally stood in the litter of the large room on the third floor of the only multi-floor building inside the rather large, walled compound.

From the scattered glass fragments on the floor and the nature of the gaping hole in the wall it seemed obvious to him the window had been blown inward while the opening had apparently been blown outward, which was a very strange event indeed. He couldn't detect any sign that explosives had been used. Daniel stood and peered out the large opening and thought about everything that he had heard in his many conversations with the local inhabitants of the nearby town.

They told him that the group that had lived here were a rather small and quite strange religious organization whose primary belief seemed to have revolved around the reality of witches who they felt were, in and of themselves, evil.

Many of the people Daniel had talked with had told him that all this destruction had been a military operation of some sort only none of them had direct knowledge of what had actually occurred out here, only the aftermath. It had happened late at night, apparently. Then the area had been blocked off and a large number of trucks had removed the bodies and anything else that was wanted and drove away. It was some time before a few individuals became brave enough to come and look. Most didn't return for a second look,

Some of those that Daniel had talked with had told him of a soft-spoken stranger with a peculiar name who asked lots of questions and took copious notes. This man had told various of the local folk that he was mostly interested in angels and not in witches at all. From what Daniel had learned this interest in angels was much like his group's interest in vampires and werewolves. Daniel knew that angels, as a type of being, had come into the mythological world in Zorastrian Persia ca. 1,500 B.C. and not, as most folk today believed, from Christianity.

He shrugged. His group believed that there was a small population in some isolated region or another whose behavior and mannerisms had given rise to the vampire and werewolf mythology which occurred much later in time and, in mostly eastern Europe, than the angel beliefs. But he couldn't see how the behavior of any group of individuals could possibly give rise to a belief in angels. But his curiosity was bubbling up even stronger. It might be interesting to explore that idea in greater detail.

Arizona.

Doma Sparta sat on the rust red soil, legs dangling over the edge of the dry river bank, and ate his lunch.

Sitting not too far away, his companion and guide did the same thing.

Doma smiled at his companion and stared out over the

empty wash and out into the space before them, rust red landscape stretching into the distance. And thought of how truly interesting his life had become.

He was now engaged in a task for a population that almost no-one knew existed. All their history was oral and passed along, if someone thought to do that, mainly inside the family, what they called the "house." Doma had been asked to do this task, to make a written history from those oral histories. It was a work to preserve the knowledge of their past and of their existence so it would not, could not, be lost.

He had taken on this chore willingly. To him, a historian of the unique, it was a good thing to do, a thing that ought to be done.

The population that he was studying, writing down, was thousands of years old, as old as humanity, stretching into the past far beyond modern man and any written document. This history, passed along, reached almost as far back in time as that point when the evolutionary path leading to Homo sapiens had split, one of the splits into several divergent populations, most of whom had disappeared. This population had not. They had survived and changed as did their "cousins," becoming two populations, two sub-species, living side by side, one unknown to the other. He was writing about the unknown one.

Doma had read the accounts, recently written down at the direction of the one that had set him on his new path and occupation, of a great cultural upheaval within this unknown population. This event had created a culture widely divergent from the Homo sapiens systems of thought and behavior. It was called "The Great Straightening" and started the deeply held tenant that house should not attack house and that every house was an autonomous entity. Over time each house developed skills and values unique to themselves, what they had come to call "house skills." They had also come to hold strong cultural values that any that tried to tell another how to live, or tried to interfere with them, would suffer, in most cases, a terminal penalty.

Yet, many houses were interlinked in mutually advantageous ways and held a common culture.

This population was quite small and widely scattered, the bulk living in mostly empty, or isolated, parts of the world although some lived close to or inside populations of "The People" as they called the others.

The few that had studied the spilt from the line leading to Homo sapiens felt that it had been a mutation of some sort which, over time, had itself mutated a number of times as the new population grew. They, over time, had inherited abilities that no member of the human population had. They had no idea how they could do what they did but accepted it as just being part of being alive, like breathing or having your heart beat.

So, Doma sat there and ate his lunch and thought, once again, how lucky he was to be doing what he was doing, writing the history of the most amazing and unknown population that trod the surface of the planet.

Wyoming.

He had slipped, for a number of miles, and a number of hours, ever so slowly and ever so carefully in the blackness of night across the fields that stretched to the far horizons from where he had parked. Now he sat in the tall grass and the darkness and listened for anything that was not just the normal night-time sounds of nocturnal animals going about their business. His eyes had long since become acclimated to the moonless night in an area that had no dwellings for miles in all directions other than the one that he was now watching. In all directions the night sky seemed to have stars that were very bright. It was quite different than where he lived.

The dwelling that he was watching had no lights showing at any window. So he waited, still as still. Finally satisfied at the lack of sound from that structure he began a slow and careful approach to the outbuilding set some distance from the ramshackle house. There was a faint light showing in the window on the side of the structure that he was slowly creeping toward.

Aerial photos had shown that the outbuilding was as badly weathered as the house. But the tire tracks leading to this place were quite new. It has taken quite an effort to locate this place in spite of everything that he had known.

He stood and listened and breathed ever so softly as he stood next to the ill-fitting door with the faint glow below the bottom edge. He heard nothing but the silence of late night.

His left hand reached out and slowly, slowly, slowly turned the door knob. He paused, took a deep breath, gently exhaled, and burst inside, spinning and ducking, firing five times.

He crouched and listened, and waited, gun aimed at the black rectangle of the outside night.

Then he straightened up, put the gun into its holster, stepped over to the large man bound to the wooden chair that was fastened to the floor, and reached out.

"This is going to hurt." He jerked the duct tape from the man's face and mouth.

The man smiled. "Not too bad. Cut me loose."

He nodded as he cut the multiple cords and said to the prisoner, "We were supposed to handle this problem, this very sensitive problem, with a gentle touch and with kid gloves, so to speak, and to tippy-toe very, very carefully. And that no-one, absolutely no-one, was supposed to know of our involvement."

Finally freed from his multiple bounds, the large man heaved himself to his feet and stretched. "Guess no-one told those five guys."

His rescuer nodded. "My truck is parked some miles from here. Shall we go? It is a nice night for a quiet walk. It reminds me of other days."

The large man laughed as they walked from the shed and into the blackness after turning off the one low wattage light fixture. The two of them had known each other since grade school, graduation from several colleges, and had traveled together around the world for a few years, having "adventures."

Maine.

The log cabin was at the end of a very long and a very twisting and a very narrow dirt road. A rather dirty, crew cab pickup truck was parked near the building.

The cabin was modest in appearance and had been there a very long time. And over that very long time the different owners had made changes and additions as the mood struck them which resulted in a rather haphazard arrangement.

The end result was that the cabin sprawled in various directions, a bedroom here and a bedroom there. But in spite of this, or perhaps because of this, it was a friendly feeling place.

The well worn furniture was comfortable rather than decorative. Depending upon which room you were in, the walls seemed to have a slight tilt in a different direction than the other rooms.

The roof was tight as were the outside doors and windows with nary a leak of water in the summer nor snow in the winter. The outside wood of this structure and the color of the metal roof made the structure blend into its forest setting.

Janeson Antzonon, whose last name was pronounced Ahn-tzo-non and whose first name was pronounced Jan-eh-son, somehow always wound up with the nickname of Ants, and Ziaza Sowden were sitting on the front porch watching evening arrive.

They had come up here a few days ago having returned from an ultrarun Trail Run in Colorado called The Leadville Trail 100, a rugged 100 mile run through the high mountainous country.

She had waited at the start/finish line while Jan disappeared into the distance with all the other trail runners in the event. Eventually the runners reappeared in a long strung out line. Jan was one the several who crossed the starting mark well ahead of the rest. A number of spectators were shouting, "Go, Ants, go!"

Now they were here, relaxing. Jan had done a lot of sleeping and eating over the past few days but was now feeling rather perky and ready for another run or two.

The cabin belonged to Ralph and Sandra Fredrickson whom they had both met almost a year ago. Ralph had given Ziaza a spare key and Sandra had given her an open invitation to use the place when ever she felt the need to have some peace and quiet.

So they were here, enjoying the piece and the quiet.

Jan was tall and lean. He was tall because his parents were tall. He was lean because he liked to run.

Ziaza was shorter than him by a good foot or so. She was slim but not from running.

Jan was just rather average looking.

She was not. Her hair was black, her brown eyes were so dark that they appeared to be black as well. Her skin was a light tan. The face was just a little round with high cheek bones and somewhat oval eyes.

Jan always looked relaxed and comfortable. His face was open and friendly, which helped him when he was in his part-time reporter mode.

She, in bearing and manner, seemed to say that she was in control. Their personalities had meshed in some strange way and complimented each other. It had been a mutual, but rather pleasant, surprise.

"Well, Jan, it is time for me to return to the work-a-day world and to make some money."

He nodded and looked disappointed and sad.

"What?" She reached across the table and grabbed one of his hands.

He sighed. "Welllllll."

She smiled. "We can have dinner at my place, drink a little wine, and, ummmmmm, talk. O.K.?"

He nodded. "Sure."

They cleaned the cabin, what little was required, and stacked what they had brought next to her truck. While she made a final check and locked up, he loaded everything.

Then the truck headed down the narrow, twisting dirt road in the usual cloud of dust. She was driving.

Back to the work-a-day world.

Maryland.

The dining room was paneled in dark wood with wide molding. The thick rug was a deep burgundy. The variable lighting in the room was set at a level pleasing to the eyes. The chairs set around the polished wood table were comfortable with plush cushions and backs. All in all, it was a very relaxing room for lovely meals, delicious desserts, and very nice after dinner libations.

Now, the six of them, three couples, The Council as they had named their group, using a name that signified nothing, had finished dinner and were now relaxing over dessert and sipping at their favorite beverages in the dining room. It was large enough to handle three couples and a few guests.

They were a very special and a very privileged and a very unknown group, other than by name, that was a part of the complexity of national security.

Ralph was the Director of The Council and the only one known to his boss, the President of The United States. Their charter kept them in existence regardless of who or what party happened to temporarily occupy the White House. Ralph could, and did, as he decided, walk into the White House and talk with The President, day or night. The staff, the Secret Service, and all the rest knew this. Everyone wondered why but only he and The President knew the reason.

Each of the other five swung great weight and authority within their respective organizations. While Ralph was known, face to face, with the President, the others were merely shadows unknown as far as the affairs of The Council were known. Their charter was quite specific. The Council was given to them by the President those rare and serious problems that were difficult to solve, that is, they were given to Ralph and he decided whether they would solve them as well as the manner, the methods, and the timing, if they did it. It was totally up to The Council to work in whatever way they deemed appropriate. They could not be questioned, they could not be second-guessed, they could not be de-funded. Given these parameters, they all were very serious about their job.

They were meeting in the home of Ralph and Sandra Fredrickson. Their house looked, more or less, like all the other houses in this area of moderately-sized, moderately priced houses. The neighbors thought that Ralph and Sandra were a nice couple, quiet and well mannered, who often had a few friends over for dinner.

No one, other than the six people concerned, knew that this house, during its extensive remodeling, had become unlike any other house in the area.

No sound could escape the house, either human or electronic other than those specifically allowed. No ears, either human or electronic, could hear anything that happened inside the house including telephone conversations or any other device currently residing there.

The grass was neatly trimmed, the house was always well maintained.

All in all, it was just one house among all the others with neatly trimmed lawns and well maintained exteriors.

The homes of Charles and Prentice James, and, Randy and Anabelle Anders had the same features as this house. It came with the job.

"Soooooo," said Ralph, looking at Charles, whose face still had quite a red streak across his cheeks and mouth. Charles was Ralph's *number two* in this special group.

Charles topped up his glass from a handy large can, tapped a few grains of salt on top of the thick white foam, took a sip, and smiled.

"Rumor control." He laughed. "I heard one and went to see if there was anything to it." He shrugged.

"Those five were just muscles for hire. From the conversations, such as they were, while they waited, they had been paid to snatch anyone looking into that rumor and were sitting way out there in the boonies waiting for someone to tell them what to do next." He laughed. "They were discussing who would dig the large hole in that rundown corral."

He looked at Ralph. "There is a leak somewhere. They were hired after I started looking around. They didn't know who I was or why I was looking around and why I had to be snatched, just that someone was willing to pay them a lot of money to see that it was done. As well as to dispose of the body when told to do so."

"Oh," said Ralph.

Randy took a sip from his very old brandy. "I will look into that." He nodded at Charles. "Be glad for tracking devices."

Vermont.

He drove slowly down the very pleasant road in this rather small town carefully checking the house numbers. His research staff had provided him a folder with copies of a number of newspaper articles and a very extensive writeup of the author and his address.

Finally, right at the edge of town, he found it, surrounded by large and very old trees.

It was a small, two-story house with a wide front porch. The white paint had faded into an almost grey. He parked, walked over and onto the porch, noting the heavily used mountain bike leaning against the house wall, and knocked on the door.

In a moment the door opened.

"Yes?" The question came from a tall and lean young man with an expectant look on his face.

His visitor smiled at him.

"My name is Daniel Fanzle. I read a number of your articles about that religious group that believed in witches. May I talk to you about that?"

"Oh. Sure." The door swung in and wide. "Come on in. Care for some tea? I was just making a pot."

"Thank you." Daniel followed him through a small living room to the kitchen in the back of the house, noting the usual clutter of someone who lived alone.

Daniel took a seat at the kitchen table while his host filled two cups and set them on the white surface. He took a sip. "You are the trail runner called Ants?"

"I prefer Jan." Jan sat, frowned at his visitor, and picked up his cup. "So, why are you interested in those articles?" He slumped and took a sip from his cup.

Daniel took another sip from his cup and thought that this was a very good tea. "I read somewhere that the force of irrational and mythological thinking often has a compelling attraction for the uneducated and the educated."

Jan nodded. "Including you?"

"No." Daniel smiled. "For me it is curiosity, not attraction." He opened the folder he had placed on the table and tapped the pages. "These are copies of the articles that you wrote. Nothing mentioned what happened to that group and their compound."

Jan nodded. "I wasn't there when what ever happened, happened. So, I had nothing to write about."

Daniel held out his cup and waited while Jan reached over, grabbed the pot, and refilled the cup. "Do you know anything else about them other than what was in the articles that you wrote?"

"Yep."

"What? If you would?"

Jan shrugged. "That bunch truly believed that witches did exist in this day and age. They believed that witches did strange things at night in rituals by torch or candle light. They believed that witches either called up demons or were directed by demons to do evil deeds. My editors felt stuff like that was a little over-the-top for inclusion in my articles."

Daniel sipped. "Did they ever see a witch?"

Jan shrugged. "They made such a claim."

"But offered no proof?"

"Nope." He shrugged. "Not to outsiders, at least."

Jan poured just a trickle of milk into his tea.

"I was told that there was another person that visited that small town and was asking about that group."

"Wouldn't be surprised. It is, or was, quite a mystery." Jan studied Daniel's face. In spite of the apparent interest Daniel showed or his smile, it was a real poker face, not giving away anything. Jan wondered if this guy was a politician of some kind.

Daniel closed his folder and leaned back. "Tell me about trail running. I know little beyond the term."

So Jan did. And as he did, he memorized Daniel's face.

Washington, D.C.

The phone on Charles' desk buzzed. He picked it up and punched the button that was pulsating red.

"What?"

He listened. And laughed.

"Send her right along."

He leaned back in his chair, coffee mug in one hand and waited. And admired the landscape painting hanging on one wall.

The door opened and she was ushered in.

"Bit of a surprise." He smiled at her. "What's up?"

Ziaza sat, grabbed the coffee container from the tray on the desk, took a cup, and poured it full. "My question exactly." She took a sip.

"Gonna explain?"

She opened the thin case she was carrying and withdrew a drawing and several pages of notes. "Jan gave me this and thought you ought to know." She took a careful sip of the very hot coffee.

Charles set down his mug and pulled everything to his side of the desk. "These are Jan's notes of his conversation and a drawing of his visitor," she explained.

Charles looked up. "Jan made the drawing?"

"Uh huh."

"A very good drawing."

"I was surprised. He never mentioned he could do that."

Charles rapidly read Jan's notes. "Well, well. I wonder who this guy is."

"Why I brought you this stuff. Thought that you could worry about it instead of Jan or me."

He laughed. "O.K. I can do that."

She stood. "Thanks."

Charles leaned way back in his chair. "No problem. I hope." He shrugged and laughed. That laugh said that he truly enjoyed what he did for a living.

New Mexico.

Far out in the solitude of the empty space of mountains and valleys, with few roads of any kind, they had a place on land that had been bought many years ago. It was a land of greys and browns.

The group lived a quiet life and bothered no-one.

The neighbors, few and far between, thought that it was a retreat of some sort or other, but not one of those "hippy" things left over from the 1960's, for the inhabitants dressed in plain clothes colored a soft brown and were quiet and withdrawn. These folk bought all their supplies in the nearby towns, nearby meaning that it was only a few hours drive, one way, to do that.

The inhabitants were, unknown to their neighbors, members of an ancient order with other small establishments scattered here and there in various parts of the world. This place was now the hub of their organization, the place where they slowly gathered information. It was read and re-read and analyzed and discussed. While this establishment had been utilized for a few generations, the greater group stretched back in time for a number of centuries.

They referred to themselves as "The Searchers," those who sought the truth behind the writings of the solitary soul that had filled the slim volume from which they all took their direction, their purpose, and the ultimate reason for their existence.

Now they had a visitor, a very rare occurrence.

Daniel Fanzle was ushered inside, led down a long dim hall, and into a small room, the office of The Director of The Order.

The elder stood and shook Daniel's hand.

"I am Frederick Hondon." He grinned. "What you might called The Head Tiger." He sat and waggled one hand at Daniel. "Sit, sit. Refreshments will arrive shortly."

Daniel sat. And waited.

Hondon nodded. "You have come here to ask questions, no doubt."

Daniel nodded. "Yes, I did."

Frederick nodded back. "Sooooooo?"

"I would like to speak to one of your, ummm, members, if I may?"

"Certainly." Frederick smiled. "Which one?"

"Doma Sparta."

Frederick's smile fell apart. He shook his head. "Not possible!"

"Why not?"

"He is not here."

Daniel leaned back in his chair and took a sip of orange juice from his glass. The refreshments had arrived. "Oh. May I leave my card and have him contact me whenever he returns?"

Frederick slowly shook his head.

Daniel stood. "Ah well." He set his glass on a small table.

"SIT!" snapped Frederick.

Daniel dropped back into his chair, frowning. He didn't appreciate having orders barked at him.

"It is not what you might think. Be patience and I will explain."

Daniel nodded. And slumped. Just a little. He reached over and took another sip of orange juice.

Frederick pulled a thin volume from a patch pocket on his jacket and cleared his throat, opened it and read the first sentences.

"Once upon a time in the long ago past. It happened. A wise man saw an angel."

He looked up. "My order has been collecting bits and pieces of information, or tales, for several thousand years, searching for that reality. Now, I do not believe in angels, or demons, or witches. As Doma pointed out, just recently, that has been an error in our belief and a waste of thousands of years. It was a discussion that Doma made in his most recent notes which I believe to be most correct."

"Doma was, is, a very good observer. I believe as did he, now, that there is a group of some kind, out there somewhere, who favor dark clothes, and who seem to have, ah, special skills."

"Angels?"

"Yes. We call them that, but have no idea what they call themselves. We now think that Doma was very close to finding the truth."

"He was?" Daniel sat straighter.

Frederick nodded. "When Doma, ah, disappeared, we cleaned his room and put what little was there in storage, just in case he ever returned."

"How close?" Daniel leaned forward. "Disappeared?"

"Doma was one of the best researchers we have ever had. He had an instinct for finding information that others couldn't. He kept detailed notes. All left behind in his room. He stated in those notes, mostly to himself, that he thought that the author D. Grant knew much more about what he was researching than she was willing to tell him. He stated that he was going to seek her out and to try, um, to learn more."

"But he didn't?"

"No. He disappeared."

Daniel stared at him.

Frederick sighed.

Daniel waited.

Frederick cleared his throat. "Let me explain that. Doma, when he was resident, would always take an early morning walk before most of us were awake."

He cleared his throat again. "On the day that he disappeared, after he had been gone far too long, two of our members followed his footsteps along the game trail that meanders across the valley floor, the one he always took his walks on, to, um, find his body. We assumed that he had a heart attack, or something like that. So they thought to bring the body back. However . . . "

"Ummmm," prompted Daniel, leaning forward a bit

more.

"Way out there," Frederick waved one arm, "his footsteps stopped and it appears that he turned around. There were another set of footprints, smaller footprints facing his. But these footprints came from nowhere. That is, there were no similar footprints leading to that spot." His eyes watched Daniel's face carefully.

"From the placement of their footprints, it appears that Doma sat on a large rock as did the other. Doma moved his feet about. The other didn't. Next to these other footprints the two who searched felt that they could see an impression in the dust like the bottom of a pack, or knapsack."

"And . . . ?"

"Those footprints didn't leave that spot. Nor did Doma's. Neither of them walked away from there."

Daniel sighed.

"I know," said Frederick. "But true." He sighed even heavier than Daniel. "We think that he got too close to the truth, somehow."

"Too close?"

"As I said, we have been seeking for several thousand years. Perhaps the angel didn't wish to be found."

"And took him to that end?"

Frederick nodded. "Because we have Doma's notes, we will try to backtrack everything that he did. Perhaps we may find the same thing, or things, that he did. Only we hope to be much more careful."

Daniel nodded and stood. "I do appreciate you talking with me."

Frederick stood. "But you don't believe it."

Daniel laughed. "Actually I do, I really do." He shrugged. "However, like you, I will try to be much more careful."

He looked into Frederick's eyes. "Is there anything that I can do for you?"

Frederick took one of Daniel's hands in his. "No. But. It is our secret."

"Safe with me, Frederick, safe with me."

"Travel safe, then." He watched Daniel walk down the hall. "Travel safe."

Washington, D.C.

Charles and Randy met in Randy's company cafeteria.

It looked like a standard cafeteria. Overhead there were bright florescent lights. The floor was covered with non-ceramic tile of some sort in alternating blue and grey squares. The walls were painted soft yellow. All the tables were small, with dark brown tops, surrounded by four chairs. The serving area was the usual stainless steel with a slid-your-tray-along rails in front.

But the food was different. It was why Charles preferred to meet Randy here for lunch. The selection ranged from Italian to Chinese to Thai and things in between. The several chefs had been lured away from some of the best restaurants in the area, after proper vetting, of course.

Today Charles had taken the Thai dish, telling the server that a 4 on the scale of heat 1-5, with 5 being the hottest, would be just fine.

Randy, as he often did, had a great leafy salad of some sort with a number of additional ingredients added to it.

Charles chewed, swallowed, and puffed air through his mouth. "Great food!" He took a swallow of his beverage from his large glass. The beverage was dark brown with a thick creamy head. One could get just about anything in beverages as well.

He looked across the table at Randy. "O.K., what'cha find

out?"

"A very slippery customer."

Charles nodded and took another swallow of his beverage.

"Daniel Fanzle is a very, very, very, carefully created facade."

"But?" prompted Charles.

Randy smiled at him. "Given the skill, and the money, that it took to do that, it really raised questions as to who we were looking for."

Charles leaned forward, slid thick forearms onto the table. "Something we need to be worried about?"

Randy laughed, softly.

Charles frowned. "Nuff games. Who is this guy?"

"Ever hear of Bandersnatch Endeavors?"

"The mega-bucks privately owned company that seems to find clever ideas and things before anyone else?"

Randy nodded and stuffed some of his salad into his mouth.

Charles stood, walked away, and returned with a bigger glass, brimming with the dark beverage. As he sat, Randy said, "He is the one that owns it."

"My, my. And he is poking around in that nutzy religious thing?"

"Seems so."

"Think that I ought to have a talk with him? Ask Ralph?"

"Ahhhhhh, no." Randy shook his head.

He slid a thick folder across the table which he had removed from his ever present brief case. The worn cover of the folder was stamped with every type of security clearance that there was with two additions.

Charles stared at it, then at Randy. "Am I going to get

shot, or suddenly disappear, if I touch that thing?"

"Have no fear." Randy pulled a single piece of paper from his brief case and slid it across the table. "Just sign on the bottom line."

Charles did.

Randy smiled at him. "Now be surprised."

Charles opened the folder and began to read. As he read his focus became so strong that the cafeteria disappeared, all surrounding noise faded away, there was nothing else but the burning questions forming in his mind that required answers.

New Mexico.

Daniel Fanzle sat at an outside table of one of the restaurants that he enjoyed and took another bite from the wonderful assortment on his plate.

Then he opened the folder just delivered to him by one of his ever efficient staff, Hank Schmidt, a very clever person, as were all this staff.

Well, well, well, he thought, how did I ever attract their attention. Of course they had followed his career, his new career. That was a given. But nothing should have caused this.

He finished his meal, paid, and left, to visit some of the local art galleries. He needed to think about the most recent past. Buried in there, somewhere, he had tripped over something that had gotten their attention.

As he wandered abstractly through the third gallery his curiosity grew stronger and stronger. Angels, vampires, and werewolves. What was there about those things that had caused all this attention from that bunch? Surely not witches?

He pointed at a painting and bought it.

Strolling down the street, painting tucked under one arm, he decided that he needn't worry. Mainly because he knew how they operated and he knew that he couldn't do anything about it anyway.

As he carefully placed the painting on the rear seat of his car, his staff member, the one that had delivered the message, stood nearby, waiting.

"Hi, Hank."

Daniel told him, in detail, what he wished, and watched his man wander down the street and merge with the tourists that were going from here to there and elsewhere.

Daniel headed for his next destination.

Vermont.

Ziaza Sowden was lounging in her pajamas, in the early morning light, on her rear deck, sipping coffee and watching the birds jump about.

She considered this the very best part of any day. Quiet and comfortable.

Her phone rang, interrupting the quiet.

She picked it up, looked at the display, and laughed.

The display read: "Good Morning, Ms. Phelps, we have a mission, if you choose to take it."

"Hi, Charles, what do you want? Pretty early in the day for this."

He laughed. "Washington, D.C., the city that never sleeps, so to speak. You and your's doing anything?"

"No. Everyone is on a little R'n'R."

"Got a big bucks job for you, Ziaza."

"Doing?"

"What you do best. Watching. Research of a, ah, special kind." She heard him take a sip of something.

"All right. Who and when?"

He laughed. And coughed. "Oooops. Never laugh with

your mouth full."

She heard him take another sip of something.

"O.K.," he said, after clearing his throat. "I already sent everything you need to your computer. Here's the decode code." He carefully told her, slowly, so she could write it down and not make a mistake. "Four people way at the top of the political pecking order. One, or more, of them did something very not nice to the President. I'll tell you what, but only face to face, if you want to know."

She sat up. "That sensitive?"

"You betcha. And then some! Taking the job?"

"Two days to round up my troops and get started. That good?"

"Ka-Ching!"

"Huh?"

Charles laughed, a loud happy sound. "That was the sound of the cash register stuffing a big bunch into your account. Send reports as you see fit. Ahhh . . . "

"What?"

"This is a job related to a project that Ralph accepted. So, anything that you might need is available."

"I will let you know. If. O.K.?"

"Take care."

"Always, Charles, always."

"Bye, then." He hung up.

She disconnected, then dialed two numbers, one after the other, and left the same message. And slumped in her chair.

And enjoyed the early morning and sipped her coffee. And watched the birds jump around.

Two days later she added a few additional items to her ready pack, snatched it up and walked into the garage.

As she passed down the narrow street and one of her

neighbors, she waved and honked her horn three times.

He waved back, and would watch her place until she returned.

The Big City. The Main Office.

He walked into the office of RoundAbout Publishing, stopped at the correct desk, and waited.

She looked up.

"I have an appointment."

"Name?"

He told her. She nodded and pushed a button.

"Daniel Fanzle is here."

The intercom made strange noises.

"Go right in." She pointed at the large mahogany door.

He walked over and pushed it open.

"Come in," boomed a large voice from a large, rather unkempt man half-rising from his chair. "Take a seat." He waggled one hand at the several chairs and dropped back into his.

Daniel closed the door and sat in the middle one facing the desk.

"Sooo, how can I help you?"

"I would like to hire one of your authors for a special project."

"Ah huh. Who?"

"D. Grant."

The man leaned back, then rocked back and forth, convulsing with laughter. Tears ran down his cheeks. Finally, he sucked in a deep breath, wiped his eyes with materials from a handy box, blew his nose, and stared at Daniel.

Daniel waited. He had never encountered a reaction like that before.

"D. Grant," rumbled the publisher, mostly to himself. "Oy vai!"

"A problem?"

"Such a problem I wouldn't wish on my mother-in-law." He shrugged. "So maybe I would."

"Immmmm. She has written a number of books for you."

"True."

"Then?"

He sighed. "You can't hire her."

"Why not?"

"Because no one can hire her."

Daniel stared at him. "You do."

"Nope!"

Daniel cleared his throat and began to wonder whether he had come to the correct office.

The publisher leaned forward, stomach pressing against the edge of his desk, and stared at Daniel. "So bubee, it works this way. And you ain't gonna believe it, believe you me!" He sucked in a deep breath. "D. Grant and her associate waltz into my office, unannounced, drop a finished manuscript on my desk, tell me, the publisher, how they want things handled, receive a large bundle of cash, always cash, and waltz out, usually laughing happily."

He leaned back and sighed. "I sell lots of her books. So I'm happy, she's happy, and her readers are happy. My doctor says that I can get an ulcer from handling Ms. Grant. BUT! I go home and yell at my wife, so I don't. My wife understands. So she is happy also."

He leaned back into an upright position and tapped the desk top with one fingertip. "So you see, bubeleh, you can't hire her unless you want to wait until whatever happens, happens."

Daniel nodded and stood. "Thank you for your time."

A large hand waggled at him. "Time I have got a lot of."

Daniel closed the door and headed for the outer door. He noticed a woman at a rear desk pick up a phone and make a call.

On the way down in the elevator, Daniel's memory fetched up the name.

"Even stranger," he said to himself, he being the only person in the elevator.

He had just tripped over another wire. Now their curiosity would be rising to higher levels. It was time to go home and work on something else, at the same time.

Maryland.

The shafts of morning sunlight that poured through the kitchen windows made bright squares on the floor, and tickled her bare feet.

Ralph and his adopted daughter Sandrel, sat and watched his wife Sandra making breakfast. It was her feet that got tickled. She didn't notice.

Neither of the watchers offered to help as both knew that Sandra preferred to do the cooking by herself.

As she gave the scrambled eggs a last stir, the front door banged open and slammed shut.

"Oh boy, breakfast," laughed Charles as he walked into the kitchen.

Ralph pulled over another chair.

They all knew about and were mystified by Charles' ability to turn up just as a meal was being finished.

"Get a plate," ordered Sandra, smiling at Charles. "I made lots."

The four of them demolished breakfast.

"So, how you doing, kiddo?" asked Charles as he finished the last piece of toast heavily layered in raspberry jam.

"Fine," replied Sandrel, standing. Charles asked her the same question every time. "Time to take a walk." She headed for the front door followed by Shadowfog, her black German Shepherd. She bent, hooked on the leash to Shadowfog's collar, and called, "Bye, Charles." And headed out for their walk.

"Ahhhh," said Ralph, holding out his cup so Sandra could refill it.

"Our boy visited Dee's publisher and wanted to talk to him about something which caused great peals of laughter from the publisher.

"Our boy?"

"A.k.a. Daniel Fanzle."

"What is he up to? Any idea?"

"Nope?"

"Sure?"

Charles nodded. "He always did things this way. Apparent random behavior up to the moment he walked in and laid it all out on someone's desk. He frightened a lot of our own folk doing things like that."

"That why he, ah, retired at such a young age after such a short, but amazing, career?"

Charles laughed. "Not really."

"Oh?"

"He stated that he was bored and needed to do something that was more interesting."

Washington, D.C.

Timothy Grimble strode down the hall humming a contented song to himself. It was a good day, this day, even this early in the day. It was one of several good days in a row. More than several actually. Today he wore a yellow tie.

Swinging the door wide, he stepped into his offices. His

secretary, as always there before he arrived, smiled at him, stood and handed him a stack of messages, and a number of envelopes still unopened.

He took them, smiled back, poured himself a cup of coffee, a morning ritual for him, and entered his space, a large room with windows along one side framing a view of sun-drenched neatly mown grass. And the city beyond.

Stepping behind his desk, he sat and swivelled around to face the window, took a sip from his cup, leaned forward and set the cup on the window sill, and began to read the messages, dropping them, one by one, into the paper shredder.

Taking another sip from his cup and returning it to its place on the sill, he began to open the envelopes, ripping the flap with one finger. He carefully read each one and then added them to the others in the shredder.

Holding his cup in one hand, he leaned back, both feet on the window sill. And thought to himself, the best-laid schemes o'mice an' men gang oft agley. Good old Robert Burns. He shrugged, Old Bobbie didn't have the resources that he did. Ah, well, that little glitch would lead nowhere. Just a minor inconvenience.

Swivelling around he tapped a few keys, popping open a window on his computer screen and sent a carefully worded e-mail.

Massachusetts.

Swift Nicky Tanagal looked at the large man sitting in the large chair on the other side of his desk.

"True?" Swift's eyes watched the other's face.

"Yes."

Swift leaned back, picked up one of the several phones on his desk and spoke to whoever was on the other end, hung up, and waited.

In a short moment the door to the room opened and two men walked through, shut the door, and waited.

Swift Nicky Tanagal told them what he wanted done.

The large man stood, turned, and the three of them walked from the room, gently closing the door behind them.

Swift looked at the door and smiled. Sometime after lunch they would return and he would settle that problem.

Washington, D.C.

"Nice duds."

Charles smiled at Ziaza, dressed all in soft grey. He shoved a carafe and a cup across the desk at her. "Coffee?"

She sat, filled the cup, took a sip, and slid a thick folder over to him. "Here you go."

"It has only been two weeks."

She shrugged and took another sip. "Three are good guys. One is bent."

"Oh, boy," grumbled Charles as he opened the folder and began to read the materials it held.

Ziaza reached over and spread the photos out. "Here he is walking down the street carrying nothing. Here he is sitting at an outside table drinking coffee. Here is Harold Tridler, the lobbyist, stopping at his table carrying a folded newspaper. Here they are talking over coffee. Here is Tridler leaving, the newspaper still on the table. Here is Timothy leaving, holding the still folded newspaper. Here he is taking something from it and then stuffing it in his coat pocket. Here he is tossing the newspaper in the trash can. In two weeks, this happened three times. There are three bundles of photographs with dates and times."

"Timothy Grimble," grumbled Charles. "The most Senior

Staff person."

Ziaza took another bundle of photos and opened it.

"Harold Tridler meeting with Rasto Hardy. Same game with the newspaper. Twice with Rasto."

She jerked out some sheets stapled together. "Rasto Hardy is well known for snatching people who are supposed to be safe from things like that. Nothing proven, of course."

She jerked another bunched of stapled sheets from the pile. "Harold's fortune and well-being are tied to a certain large business who has had a number of upper echelon personnel put in jail, courtesy of the President urging his Attorney General to investigate that outfit. All their government contracts were yanked as well."

She tapped one of the paper stacks she had flipped open. "Harold has several well-paid politicos singing sad songs about free enterprise, the free market, and what a bad guy the President is for doing things like that. They are all trying to swing some very large contracts to that same business."

Ziaza nudged another paper loose from the pile. "That outfit is one step from being bankrupt."

Charles stuffed everything back into the folder. "Great job."

She smiled at him. "Do I get to know . . . some time?" She stood, setting her cup on his desk.

Charles laughed. "Perhaps."

Massachusetts.

The thin man in the cheap suit licked his lips, a weak smile popping on and off, and squeaked, "What? Mr. Tanagal."

Swift Nicky pointed at the chair. "Sit before you collapse, Parris."

Parris Karalon sat. And relaxed, just a little. He couldn't

see the three men standing behind him, their backs to the wall, but he knew what they could do, if they were told to do it.

Swift leaned back in his chair. "I have heard an interesting story that had your name attached to it. Soooooo, I thought that you might like to tell me about that. In some detail."

Swift told him what he had heard.

Parris slumped and swallowed loudly.

"True?" asked Swift.

Parris nodded weakly and slumped even deeper in the chair.

"Truly a bad decision," suggested Swift.

Parris licked his lips. And nodded. Someone stepped up behind him. Parris stared at Swift Nicky, and cringed, waiting for the bullet to the back of his head.

"But, not exactly your fault."

Parris managed to nod again. And to hope, a little.

"Soooooooo," said Swift. "Here is what I want to know."

Virginia.

Daniel Fanzle was relaxing in the library of his home reading something that one of this staff had handed him when he had arrived home.

The first part was a very old tale about a hunter who had befriended The Spirit of The Woods.

Thran, although his name may have been something totally different, was hunting. This male of the people lived in his home at the edge of the forest some distance from where the rest of the houses huddled together, six, maybe eight, dwellings in all.

So, on that day, he was moving as quietly as he could along a game trail in the forest, some distance from his dwelling.

He was very nervous to be this far.

He had grown up hearing the stories of the forest spirits and other creatures that lived hidden here, this deep inside the forest. Everyone knew that these beings were not to be bothered. But the summer had been cooler and shorter than usual. With what food he had stored and preserved he would not survive the coming cold time that all the elders said was going to be worse than ever.

He intended to survive. So he pushed ever deeper into the forest forbidden territory. All he wanted was sufficient food to survive, nothing more. Surely even the forest spirits and the other creatures could understand that. But maybe not. The tales were unclear as to whether such beings actually cared whether he starved or not.

Suddenly he jerked to a halt, one foot still in the air, standing as still as still could be. Something was coming his way, from in front of him, on this very same game trail.

Slowly, ever so carefully and quietly, he slipped into a thick brush cluster, his green and brown clothes merging with the green and brown of all that growth. Then he waited, breathing as softly as he was capable of doing.

Slowly, slowly, it came. The creature was making a soft sound, a soft moan it seemed to him. Carefully he checked the game trail and pondered the wisdom of bolting for his life back down the narrow meandering path as fast as he could run, back the way he had come.

Then he gasped in surprise and stared, mouth hanging open.

It was a tall woman that was making the soft moaning sound. She staggered his way, using a long staff for support as she dragged one leg and hobbled as fast as she seemed to be able to go. As she came closer he could see an arrow protruding through her right thigh, her pant leg heavily stained, deep dark red on dark brown.

She stopped and looked right at him, wobbling from side to side. One of her eyes was puffy, a trickle of blood wandered from the corner of her mouth and over her chin. Her upper garment was torn. Her clothes were dirty, her one open eye wild and staring here and there and back at him.

"Help," she gasped. "Me." And collapsed into the brush screen that he was using for cover.

Thran, or whatever his name really was, was a large man. He carefully gathered her into his arms, snatched up her staff in one hand, and started out of the forest, moving as fast as he could, headed for his dwelling.

He was staggering badly by the time he kicked his door open and lurched into his small house. Carefully he laid his burden on the narrow bed on her side, the injured leg free, and closed the door, leaning her staff in a corner.

Taking his knife from his belt he cut the shaft in half and threw that piece on the nearby table. Then he sucked in a deep breath and yanked the rest of the shaft free and pitched the barbed arrow and shaft piece onto the table next to the other part.

He checked her face and leaned very close. He could feel the soft breath against his cheek. Her eyes popped open.

"Shhhh," he said straightening up. "You are safe. But your wounds need tending."

Swiftly he cut her pant leg further open exposing the bleeding wounds. Spinning away, he gathered the appropriate plant materials and started. He had done this same thing many times before for hunters and others of his clan.

Then he gently washed the dirt from her face and was surprised. No one that he knew had features like her's. He had not met anyone in the few other clans that he had visited who looked as she did.

So while he worried about who she might be, he worked swiftly and gently. Finished, he draped a cover, one of his two, over her, built up the fire, and began to heat water to make something to eat. He was really hungry and she required food to heal. And to sleep as well.

Several days passed. Thran slept on the floor. It wasn't all that much different that sleeping in the forest on the ground, which he had done many a time. The days passed mostly in silence. She seemed content to not engage in conversation. Of course, he was not one who talked very much anyway so it was no bother to him.

Then one day she surprised him.

"Help me. I must return to my house. They will be worried."

He nodded, helped her stand, and walked with her deep into the forest, down the same game trail that he been following. She used the staff. They walked slowly.

Deeper. And deeper they walked. Well beyond any distance that he had ever come.

Into a small meadow.

She pointed at another trail. "They ran from there."

He nodded and studied the ground. Even after this much time he could see where she had struggled and fought.

He looked down that trail and wondered what clan lived that way and why they would attack her. It was not the way of his clan to attack strangers. Perhaps they were marauders?

Then she led him to a spot and stepped past the growth and onto a narrow trail he would never have seen.

She led him deeper and deeper.

Into another small meadow and over to a building that

seemed to blend into and merge with the thick surrounding vegetation.

Opening a door in what had appeared to be a blank wall, she stepped inside and turned. "Do come in."

Inside, he stared. It was the largest dwelling that he had ever been inside.

Others came running. She explained to these excited folk what had happened. Then she led him to a room and fed him all that he could eat.

These must be some of the chieftains that he had heard about. They asked him a few questions and he explained why he had been walking down that trail and how he had first met her.

Then they told him that he could have all the food that he could carry and that he wouldn't ever be in need again.

And it was true.

He always had sufficient. Never too much, never enough to make others of his clan suspicious. He was just considered lucky.

And so it went.

Year. After year. After year.

He aged, grew older.

She visited him often. And never seemed to age.

So then he knew who she was. She was one of the forest spirits.

And so, one day, he told a nephew his tale. And that tale was passed on and eventually written down somewhat altered with the passage of time.

It was a tale about a brave hunter that had once met a forest spirit.

The second part of the message was about a very recent tale about The Forest Ghost.

The Forest Ghost was reported as having been seen in an area of very rugged mountains which also happened to be in the general vicinity of what was believed by Daniel's associates in that study group to be the homeland of the vampire and werewolf mythologies.

Daniel found this last bit rather interesting. He nodded to himself. This Forest Ghost's description had some similarities to that angel that the other group had been searching for as well as The Spirit of The Woods in that rather old tale. This was also rather interesting. It was a strange convergence of several mythological belief systems. Maybe he ought to take a trip, just to see, and to lower the amount of oversight that he was sure that he was currently receiving.

Massachusetts.

It was one of the older but well maintained houses. It was perched on a high spot near the shore. As Charles climbed from his truck, he could see a number of large men wearing windbreakers wandering here and there around the building.

Inside the large living room sat Swift Nicky Tanagal, lounging in a chair, dressed in very casual attire that reeked of money. He smiled at Charles and waggled one hand at the other two chairs. "Please sit."

Charles sat, slumped comfortably, and took a swallow of the beverage handed to him by one of the men.

"What? Charles?" Swift smiled at him.

"I think that Rasto Hardy took a great deal of money and made a very great mistake."

Swift nodded at his long-time friend. "I'm listening."

Charles looked around the room and nodded at all the large men standing around wearing wind breakers. "Just you and me." He dragged his chair close to Swift.

Swift nodded and they had the room to themselves.

Charles took another swallow from his mug. "One word of this leaks out and people will wind up in deep dark places they won't really want to be in."

Swift smiled at him. "No leaks from here."

Charles nodded and then slowly, carefully told him.

Swift blanched. And nodded. "A very great mistake, indeed."

"So," added Charles. "We want to solve this problem very quietly, very, very quietly, with a minimum of damage, preferably no damage at all." He shrugged. "If it can be helped."

"I see," said Swift.

"There was a lot of money changing hands."

Swift nodded.

"We just need a lead on that."

Swift leaned forward and patted Charles' knee. "If I can, I will."

Charles shoved his chair back and stood. "Thanks, buddy. We'll owe you one." He set his mug on a nearby table.

"Always good to know." Swift smiled at him.

Illinois.

The very large man, mostly muscle not fat, leaned forward and stared across the desk at the equally large individual sitting in the only other chair in his office.

"WHAT?"

"Loosen your collar, take a deep breath, and calm down."

The large man did and looked at his Number One in the organization. He was also his very long time and very best friend.

"So tell me, Rondak, how do you know?"

Rondak smiled and nodded, one very quick nod. "I was

told. Someone who needed money told me."

Rasto Hardy leaned forward a bit more and set both hands on the desk top, fingers intertwined. "Drag his sorry butt in here for a talk."

Rondak shook his head. "Can't."

Rasto hissed. "Can't? Or won't?"

"Can't!"

"Why not?"

"Someone shot a number of holes in him and dumped the body in a trash bin."

"Umm."

"That trash bin in two blocks from here!"

Rasto bounced to his feet, chair sliding violently back into the wall.

Rondak stood more slowly. "The car is waiting by the third door in the alley. Stanley is driving."

Stanley could drive through a hurricane without blinking or being bothered by it.

Rasto and Rondak hurried down a back stairway and out the appropriate door and into the waiting automobile.

Stanley hurtled the car down the alley, into a garage and out the other side of the block and into another side street.

Eventually Rondak leaned forward and gave Stanley further directions.

On the way they stopped at a digital café where Rondak sent a single e-mail.

As they cruised down the two-lane road, Rondak opened a thick folder and began to talk softly with Rasto about various of the sheets of papers and documents.

Maryland.

The dining room was paneled in dark wood with wide

molding. The thick rug was a deep burgundy. The variable lighting in the room was set at a level pleasing to the eyes. The chairs set around the polished wood table were comfortable with plush cushions and backs. All in all, it was a very relaxing room for lovely meals, delicious desserts, and very nice after dinner libations.

Charles refilled his tall glass from a large can, tapped a few grains of salt onto the thick foam, took a sip, and looked around the table.

"Rasto Hardy, his good buddy Jaime Rondak, and their driver Stanley Wilkins, have bugged out. Their car was found abandoned. No one seems to have the faintest idea of where they went."

Randy's wife, Anabelle, smiled. "They must be inside the forty-eight states. They are not leaving. Not unless someone nails Rasto in a crate and ships him as a piece of furniture. And even that is doubtful."

Ralph refilled his glass with a very deep red wine and tipped a wee bit more into his wife's glass.

"Any ideas? Any stories?" He took a sip.

"Best that we can tell," stated Prentice, Charles' wife. "Somewhere inside the United States." She poked him in the ribs with one finger.

"Yep," said Charles as he jerked. "I suspect in some rural or not very populated region. Those kinds of areas make it difficult to know or see anything. Lots of space and few folk around. There are, in many areas, lots of summer cabins, hunting lodges, things like that. No hints. Yet."

Ralph nodded and began to serve dessert, a many layered chocolate cake.

"We'll meet in a week, then."

The group ate dessert and talked about anything but the

business at hand and eventually scattered back to their homes after thanking Ralph and Sandra for everything.

The Big City. The Main Office.

Dee and Janice sat in the guest chairs and waited for the usual storm of grumbling and mumbling to blow itself out as it always did.

Dee had handed him her latest novel and explained why she felt this one had to be handled the way that she wished.

He stared at her as she did that, once again convinced that authors were an unusual breed of being, if not a merely peculiar, but a necessary part of life, especially his life. Finally, he nodded, winced a smile into place, and agreed to whatever they, Dee and her assistant, wished, and watched the two smiling characters leave his office.

As they stood and waited for the elevator to arrive, Janice looked at Dee.

"What do you think we ought to do?"

Dee smiled. "Have a good meal."

"Then?"

"We will just have a very good meal, go visit, and then go home." She looked at her companion. "Dorothy Jant is still in the office. I saw her pick up her phone as we left. It appears The Council is still keeping an eye on the place."

Janice shrugged. "Dot works for them. But sitting in that office must be quite dull."

A soft ping announced the arrival of the elevator.

The Three Villages.

The three villages were strung along the one-lane, dirt rut that passed as the road. The highest village, at the end of the not very wide valley was slightly more populated than the other two. Hence it was regarded as the social and cultural center of the meager population of the valley. There was also a large barn big enough to hold large meetings.

The folk here, in this mountainous region of eastern Europe were isolated, both in terms of their environmental setting and in terms of their attitudes. They had a low regard for "outsiders," those that did not share their cultural values and their remembered, such as it might have been, history.

In a not very long ago, a young man of promise was born in the highest village and eventually sent into the outside world to get an education.

When he returned, as all knew that he would, he had taken a new name. He now called himself Batu Khan. This was the name of a cultural hero of this isolated population. Whether this was a historical fact or not had no meaning upon the folk beliefs of the villages. Batu Khan, who lived ca. 1207-1255, was a Mongol ruler and the founder of the Ulus of Jochi, also known as the Golden Horde.

The Golden Horde was regarded as a time of historical greatness and wonder by various populations including these folks.

This young man, now in his early thirties, had great charisma and leadership. He gathered around himself a number of others who felt that what he was proposing was not only a good idea but one that offered greater wealth than any of the villagers ever hoped to see. And it seemed to them right that many young men would follow Batu Khan.

Batu organized his followers into a well trained quasi-military unit, borrowing and modifying those aspects of the past history as he felt would be best for today's reality.

The group wanted to call themselves "The Golden Horde." Batu pointed out that they were not horsemen who could lay waste to whatever they might wish and take all the treasure that was there to find.

He explained, carefully, what their name was to be. He pointed out that the term "cartouche" meant name in the ancient Egyptian hieroglyphics. As he told this and that from his studies of history he held up the Command Staff with a round-shaped device attached to the top of the shaft. This was, he explained a *shen ring*. This ring signified that they were now eternally protected. And from this time forward they would be known as The Golden Cartouche.

This would be the only name any outsider would know for their group. Anyone trying to discover from whence they had come would be unable to do so. Thus their villages would be protected.

And so, the mercenary organization known as "The Golden Cartouche" came into existence.

Other Folk

House Darthar Na.

The meadow stretched upwards from the surrounding forest in a gentle slope to the base of the many storied structure. It was half chateau, half fairytale castle. Everything was constructed of light red wood perched on heavy dark green stone foundation walls, roofs of soft brown. The whole thing stretched along the slope rather than up and down the mountain's flank.

As the pair walked along the long hall on the main floor paneled in golden oak, she laughed happily.

He looked at the paintings hanging here and there and thought, not for the first time, that it must come from her being raised as one of The People for so long.

She was the Head of House Darthar Na, and formally known as Daliera Fontala a'Anathor a'Mdator a'Zgura a'Winfa a'Relda d'Darthar Na.

He was the Head of House Darthar and Lord of the Darthar Family, and was formally known as Othara a'Anathor a'Mdator a'Zgura a'Winfa a'Relda d'Darthar. House Darthar is the oldest house of all the houses.

House Darthar is also known as The Bringer of Order; House Darthar Na as The Protector of The Innocent.

From the split, very many long ago as The Feyra recorded time, into two houses, they have remained Shadow Houses, quiet ones who do not appear to be interested in meddling in the affairs of others. But the two houses have always remained a single family, a secret, a closely held family secret. And a very useful thing, as all the other houses saw them as soft retiring and unconcerned.

It was a totally kept secret among Family Darthar that the long ago split was a deliberate maneuver that allowed each side of the family to develop their abilities independently of the other without causing undue concern among all the rest of their folk if such power had been concentrated in one House. The two houses together watched over all of their folk to protect them from harm.

House Darthar Na housed The Seven Stands of The Fontala, a warrior class called The Protectors of The Innocent from which the House took its label. In addition it housed a small group known as The Shadow Feyra which split away from the main population thousands of year before and had become nocturnal.

She pointed at this picture and that picture. "I got all of them from House Patelan."

"Ummmmm."

"You remember the tale Hofga told us?"

"Ummmm."

She laughed. And told him that tale dating from the middle of the 1700's.

He was a very successful painter of portraits in the area where he lived. One of the few. They were in high demand by those who could afford such. He was one of the very skilled, one within the few that were sought out.

Each of the skilled carefully guarded how they made the particular shades of color that marked their work as much as their signature did in one of the corners.

He was also the one that accepted students, never more than three at a time.

Potential students had to show their work to him and discuss how they painted and why they painted and what they thought he could teach them.

Most who walked into his studio seeking training were refused. He never explained why. They knew better than to ask.

Then, one sunny day, she walked into his studio, portfolio held under her left arm. She walked in with a confident stride, a determined look on her face.

He waved her to a stool while he carefully finished a tiny bit of the portrait that he was working on.

At the moment he had no students so he could spend all his time on his own work. Finally he turned on his stool and smiled at her.

"I wish to learn," she said.

He nodded and wondered from what part of the country she had come from. Her accent had something strange about it.

"It is expensive," he said.

She shrugged.

Well, he thought to himself, she has an interesting self confidence that you don't often see in a student. Maybe she even has talent?

"Show me your work. Please?"

She handed him her portfolio.

"Ask when you are done." She wandered around his studio looking at his sketches and works in progress, apparently unconcerned, while he opened and began to slowly leaf through her work. Some of her work was done in black and white, some in color. The bulk were portraits, interesting portraits. He could almost feel the presence of the face, of the individuals she had drawn.

Well, well, well, he thought, she does have talent.

He looked up. "You wish me to each you?"

"Just so." She sat on the stool near him.

"What can I teach you?"

"Color."

"Color?"

"Just so."

"Explain."

She did. In very precise terms, pointing to places on the portrait that he had been working on, discussing the interplay of color and light and shadow. Then she leaned back and waited, still as still ever could be.

For a moment he sat and stared at her. Then he nodded and smiled. "It will be my pleasure to do what I may."

She nodded, reached into a pocket, and pulled out her fist, and held it out to him. "Payment."

He held out his hand. She dropped the coins into his quickly cupped hands.

"Enough?" she asked.

He gulped and nodded. "Tomorrow? Will you be able to start tomorrow." And reached for her portfolio. And hesitated as she frowned.

"Ah, may I look at these until tomorrow?" he asked.

She nodded, stood, and walked from his studio.

Every afternoon, exactly at the same time, six days a week, she walked into his studio. And they worked. He carefully made her do this or that bit of painting, demonstrating how to make things better. And every day she did. And got better.

So he wondered about his student. He had refused everyone else that had come looking to be a student. Now he had one student, only the one student. The interesting thing to him was the realization that his work was also getting better. And not only was he getting better but that the very top tier of society and wealth were now bidding against each other for his work. His fame was spreading widely. But as his reputation grew so did the grumbling from those few painters that somehow felt they were being unfairly overshadowed by him and being under-appreciated by those that should be buying their work

Then one day, late in the summer, she walked in, ever so quiet as always, ever so self assured, sat on her stool, and pointed at one spot on his current project.

"Show me how to make a paint like that, that very bright white."

He shook his head. It was his secret, ever so carefully guarded. It was one of those things that made his work so unique.

She opened her portfolio, she always carried it, and handed him a small painting of a forest at the edge of a meadow.

"I will show you how to make this green if you will show me how to make your white." She pointed at an area that had immediately caught his eye.

He nodded, was once again, or perhaps still, amazed that such a young woman could be so talented.

They spent the entire afternoon talking about and showing each other the manufacture of those certain pigments.

Monday morning and he groaned and pushed himself upright.

He had been taken from his house, beaten, and thrown into this small room yesterday, the day when he never had guests or visitors. Two of his competitors had pooled their resources and had hired those who did this sort of work, to remove their competition.

He had no idea of where he actually was or for how long he had to live.

For two days he sat on that dusty floor and ate the food that he wouldn't have fed to a rat. He wondered when it would happen, when they would kill him, and where they would dump his body, far from where he had lived, he supposed.

It was in the middle of the night, some days later, when heavy thumping sounds came from over his head startling him awake. It was this new noise, the new different noise that had pulled him from his troubled sleep.

Now what is it this time? Were his captors preparing to kill him?

Then it became quiet, very quiet, much more quiet than it had ever been. He sighed. So, he thought, here it comes.

The door to his room slammed open. Someone walked in, holding a lantern high, followed by several others holding heavy wooden staffs.

"What they did was not nice," said his student. "Come. You are not far from your house."

He lurched upright and stared at her and her companions. "Who are they?" He pointed.

"First, Second, and Third Brothers."

Once they stepped outside the building he saw that she was correct. His house was not very far from here.

Then, over the next week or two, he heard various stories of the mysterious disappearance of two well-known artists and of the fire that badly damaged a house not too far from where he lived.

When he asked her about these things, she merely shrugged, and said that those people were not nice.

And as time passed no one talked any longer about those

happenings. Then one day she walked in and held out a closed fist and waited for him to hold out his hand. She dropped a fist full of gold coins into his open hand.

"I am done," she said. "Teacher." And started to turn to leave.

"WAIT!"

She turned back and looked at him, a slight frown creasing her brow. "Ummmm."

"I shouldn't accept this. You saved my life."

"I will see and admire more paintings, Teacher." She nodded. "Be calm. Paint beautiful. Worry not." She bowed to him, turned, and walked calmly away.

For the rest of his long career he found that, somehow, his life was calm in spite of sudden changes in his fortunes or political favor.

He told his son as he sat in a chair and spoke of his favorite student and showed his son, also a painter, how to mix certain pigments.

He no longer painted. His eyes only saw mostly blurry things and his hands refused to remain steady. Of course he had lived a long time and had done some truly beautiful work. And his son nodded as the tale was spun and worked on his own painting. And people marveled over his whites and greens.

"I had a long talk with the House Head and we agreed that I could hang all these paintings in the main hallway."

"Ummmm. Different."

"Some of the things that The People do are nice, like hanging paintings on their walls. Some of these paintings date from the time of that tale, others are later. Paintings like these are one of their house skills."

He nodded.

House Patal.

He had spent a number of weeks here, talking and writing in his journal. Daliera had been most correct in deciding to do this. Her people's oral history should be captured and written down for posterity.

He found that this activity was even more exciting than all the previous research he had been doing. And most of what he was now learning was quite intriguing. Here he was, sitting in one of the hidden houses, a rather unique aspect of their culture, and working on their history. From his past experience he had found that oral traditions usually changed over time with a bad tendency to drift into just-so stories and mythological justifications for the past as well as badly mangled poorly remembered events in the previous generations.

But, to his amazement, even though he had been told this before starting out to record everything that he could find, he had found that these folk were extremely long-lived, many, many times the span of a human life span. So, often, the oral history he was given was the first hand experience of the individual talking with him.

Doma closed his journal, one of the many he had filled, and took a sip of coffee, a cup of coffee was always offered to any visitor. It was considered the polite thing to do.

Ever since the discovery of the coffee bean had spread in the 13th Century, these folk, the ancient offshoot from the Homo sapiens line, had taken to it as a primary beverage, and had developed quite a few cultural beliefs and behaviors around it. Their physiology was such that large quantities of caffeine apparently had no affect on them at all.

And as he had slowly learned through his many visits to various of the houses, this was one of the least differences between themselves and those they called "The People." This term was often used in a very derogatory sense.

He leaned back and sighed. He was done here. He thanked their host, House Head Patal, and nodded to his guide, Hakar, Third Brother of House Darthar. This was the last of Daliera's Cousin-Houses. Now he would visit all the Sub-Houses of House Darthar. It was interesting that this was the only group that named their House after the House Head.

Patal stood and led the pair to the outside door expressing this best wishes to Daleira as well as to Doma's further work as they walked down the corridor. Patal agreed with Daliera that this endeavor was needed for the good of all their folk.

The Wild Garden. House Hinterane.

The house was located down a rather narrow lightly traveled two-lane road that ran through a mostly rolling open countryside dotted here and there with large houses set well back from the lane. All these houses were behind heavy and ornate gates set into the very high walls, up long drives, and around long curves.

This house loomed over everything from the top of the low hill. The wide, front steps led up to the large double doors, dark wood totally decorated by intricate carvings. Down the hall, beyond the doors, past several wide staircases, was a large library. All of its walls were lined with bookcases. The only furniture in this room was a table set with three chairs. On the table sat several cups and an over-sized carafe filled with coffee.

This house was a shadow-cloaked house, wrapped in grey shadow that kept it from being seen by any of their folk unless the House Head wished them to be able to see it. To The People it was just a very large house in an area that had many very large houses set back on very large holdings of land.

House Head Helsing sat at the table with his Third Daughter, Janice. He had recently bought a sizable collection of books and documents. All the materials dealt with the early mythologies of The People. Helsing was known among that small and devoted group of serious collectors for his knowledge and resources on that subject. He only dealt through the mail via several shops whose specialty was keeping anyone from back tracking to the originator of that mail. Now, Helsing and Janice were discussing the value and probable age of each of the items that he had bought. Most were of little importance or value, but some were very old. A few of these would have notices posted to the few who might be interested and could afford to purchase them.

Helsing leaned back, took a sip from his cup, and nodded. He held out a piece of paper. "Now that we are done with that, I have something that I wish you to look into. I have received inquiries from someone that I have never heard from before. This is his name and the name of his company. Find out all you can about both."

Janice took the piece of paper, read it, and stood. "I will be in my office for some time. Is this something to, ummm, worry about?"

"No. Not yet. We will discuss that after you have found whatever you can find."

A Very Large Place.

It was constructed from large black stone of various shapes. The structure was dense, compact, a gloomy looking castle with pediments and towers all along the upper walls.

Hongor lived here. No one ever used any other name. He was the only occupant. He was a member of a very ancient line. At times his form reflected that ancient line, especially when he was upset.

He sat in a large chair by a heavy wooden table and rumbled to himself. He had sent to Daliera the list of houses which she had requested, those most likely to allow their oral histories to be recorded by that people historian. It was beyond everyone's experience to have one of The People so intimately involved in such private knowledge. But Daliera had made a strong argument that this was necessary, pointing out that The Fontala, The Protectors of The Innocent, has lost one seventh of their own past when the Seventh Stand, including their own member, The One Who Remembers, the holder of their oral history, had perished in that great battle of the very long ago. She had since recreated The Seventh Stand.

Hongor had collected information in a great number of volumes dealing with every family of their small population. He listed all the families, those still alive and those that were no more, as well as the various mergers and splitting apart of the families.

Now he was bothered about something he had heard relating to the behavior of some of The People. Bright yellow eyes peered down a long muzzle, bright white canines poking down past his lower jaw, as he rumbled to himself and reread the message he had received from one of the many who sent him information.

Then he straightened up, took a sip of coffee from his large mug, and looked just like Hongor again. He would just have to wait and see what came next. At the moment there was no need to reach out to other Houses. Yet.

House Fartop.

A tall grey stone cylinder forty feet in diameter stood on a high ridge, all bare rock, cold wind blasted stone.

Aranda, House Head, stood in the uppermost circular room having four large apertures evenly spaced around the walls, open to the outside. The wind puffed in through one of the openings.

The tall man stood next to an even taller bird. It was a Tarken, very rare, highly treasured. It mostly looked like an eagle.

It was early evening. Aranda was talking with it, at times smiling, his long canines glistening in the light of the fluttering torches. In many of the houses the males inherited this physical characteristic.

Finally their discussion was over and he headed down the circular stairway.

In one of the lower rooms, he sat at a small table and began to compose the note. Finished, he reread it, nodded satisfaction, and sent it away, two copies winging through space to find Hofga and Jonathon, both very close friends.

House Darthar.

The structure flowed in graceful curves around the great meadow set deep in a dense forest. At times it seemed as if the structure was actually the forest itself.

Hofga stomped across the meadow, heavy footsteps sending shock waves across the dense grass cover, and thumped upon the outside door.

The door swung open. "Do come in, Hofga. And calm down. We don't need to do repairs to the place."

His host led the still badly agitated Hofga down a hall and into a rather pleasant room containing a small table and two chairs. Handing a filled cup of coffee to Hofga, he took the other one, sat, and took a sip.

Hofga dropped into the other chair, took a sip, and

grumbled, "You received a note from Aranda as well?"

"Yes."

"Ah umm."

"Interesting. And somewhat bothering."

Hofga took another sip and frowned.

The other nodded. "The People are always doing strange."

"Ah, dota!" Hofga held out his cup. It was refilled. "This strange could bring many of them to that place."

"We could ask Hondo, The Thing Dealer, to send a watch thing to report on whatever The People are about. They will never see it."

Hofga nodded.

House Ritilar.

It was a small rectangular structure. The first level was all large stone, partially set into the side slope of the mountain. The next level was constructed of horizontal logs, neatly dovetailed at the corners. The last level, the ends of the house, great triangular shapes of thick vertical planks, supported the great roof that hung down past the second level. The roof was thick and a soft yellow color. The outside walls, those of natural wood, were beginning to fade into a weathered grey. It looked like all the other structures in this part of the world.

Nyecol had visited the small settlement two miles down the dusty and rutted trail that passed as a road in this very isolated region deep inside the great mountain range. Her house specialized in making those implements that the local population used in their daily activities.

While she was trading, she noticed that a strange group of The People had arrived in a great vehicle capable of getting this far. They had handed over, to the only inn keeper, a rather young woman and a great sum of their money. Then they had rushed away.

Now she was trading with the local folk again, several weeks later. She noted that the young woman was still here, but being very carefully watched by the family of the inn keeper.

After she was finished and strolling up the trail toward her House, she spotted a watch thing, carefully observing the young woman and her keepers. She stared at it. It was most unusual for one of her folk to be that interested in the usual strange behavior of The People. She would mention all this to the House Head and wonder to him whether they ought to relocate.

House Darthar.

She stood in front of the outside door, a rather short female, and knocked gently, and waited. It was the polite thing to do.

She looked around at the forest setting. It was a very pleasant place. The door silently opened and he looked out.

She bowed to him.

"Here is Tineral, First Daughter of House Fartop."

"Do come in, Tineral." He stepped back and bowed.

She followed him down the interior hallway and into a small, comfortably furnished room.

He poured two cups of coffee and handed her one and waited until she sat. He sat in the chair next to her and took a sip. And waited. It was the polite thing to do.

She took a sip. And waited.

"Ummmmmm," he said.

"Lord, House Head Aranda sent me to bring a message."

"Ah, umm."

"In the long ago past, House Fartop helped House Ritilar

in a minor problem. The two houses have a relationship between them."

"Ummm." He took a sip.

"The People are doing very strange in the very small people cluster near House Ritilar. House Ritilar is very bothered and studies relocating." She took a sip. "House Head Aranda has been told of the watch thing observing The People behavior. It was seen by Second Daughter Nyecol of House Ritilar."

"Ah, umm." He nodded, and took a sip. "Hondo was asked to do that, send one of his watch things. After Aranda sent Hofga and me his first messages."

He refilled her cup then his own.

"Hongor has also sent a message. He has heard bothering from several others. It appears all a part of some pattern of very strange People behavior." He took a sip. "I will ask House Ritilar to be careful cautious, but to not relocate unless they believe it is a thing that must be done." He nodded.

She took a sip, and nodded back.

Bits and Pieces

House Hinterane. The Wild Garden.

The walls of the large room were lined with bookcases. The only furniture in this room was a table set with three chairs. On the table sat several cups and an over-sized carafe filled with coffee.

He filled two cups of coffee and handed one to Janice. And took a sip.

The pair were seated at the table.

She had several sheets of paper in a thin stack in front of herself. He took a sip.

"Ummmmmm."

She nodded. And told him what she had found.

"The company, Bandersnatch Endeavors, the name is a people joke based upon a favorite poem from a book of fantasy written by an English author, is extremely wealthy, as The People measure wealth. It is privately owned, by one person, Daniel Fanzle. He seems to be the one that wishes to buy the materials, those pieces of The People's mythologies relating to the earliest writings upon vampires and werewolves as well as items relating to angels."

She took a sip.

Helsing did the same.

"It appears," she continued, "that this person is considered among The People to be an extremely intelligent individual with a special skill. He can take disparate pieces of information and put them together in new ways that give him great insight into whatever he happens to be studying."

He nodded. "I think that we will not be selling anything to this person." He smiled at her. "Do talk with Daliera about this."

She stood, bowed, and walked from the room.

Maryland.

They were meeting in the home of Charles and Prentice.

All the rooms were much less formal in decor than the home of Ralph and Sandra.

Richlin, the daughter of Charles and Prentice, was visiting some friends.

As was the custom of the group, they had a great dinner and dessert. Now they were scattered around the living room, each if their favorite place, sipping their favorite beverage. It was time to discuss various aspects of business.

Charles looked at Ralph.

He shook his head. "Still no word as to where Rasto might be hiding."

Randy cleared his throat.

"We are going to do a deep search on everyone of the names of the people in Rasto's organization that we have, looking at property ownerships. There is some thought that he might be in someone's house, or cabin. He certainly is not in anything that he owns."

Charles smiled, and nodded. "I couldn't find out anything either." He looked at Ralph. "Think we ought to drag Tim Grimble in and have a, um, strong talk with him?"

Ralph shook his head. "We will just monitor everything that he does. So far, the information that we need hasn't turned up. If we spook him, we will never get it."

Charles topped up his glass and shook a few grains of salt

onto the think white foam. "This is getting irritating."

"The President," said Ralph, "is being very patient, given the situation."

"For how long?"

Ralph shrugged.

Randy stood. "Well, time to get busy. Before we run out of time."

The group thanked Charles and Prentice for their hospitality and scattered.

Massachusetts.

It was one of the older but well maintained houses. It was perched on a high spot near the shore. As Charles climbed from his truck, he could see a number of large men wearing windbreakers wandering here and there around the building.

Inside the large living room sat Swift Nicky Tanagal, lounging in a chair, dressed in very casual attire that reeked of money. He smiled at Charles and waggled one hand at the other two chairs. "Please sit."

Charles sat, comfortably slumped, and took a swallow of his beverage handed to him by one of the men who then vacated the premises.

"What? Charles?" Swift smiled at him.

Charles smiled back. He knew that Swift was actually his friend's name, a family tradition.

"Rasto Hardy is known as someone who can snatch folk and get them to other places."

"Indeed."

"Other countries?"

"Uh huh."

Charles leaned back and took a swallow and wiped the foam from his lip.

"You wouldn't happen to have contacts, friends, in those other countries by any chance."

Swift took a sip of the brown liquid in his glass.

"Not by chance. We do have, erm, business in a number of places."

"Sure," agreed Charles.

"So?"

"Any way you can ask around about the matter we discussed earlier. It is looking like what we seek is not inside the United States."

Swift straightened up. "No wonder Rasto is so carefully hidden. He would do better to speak with you."

Charles nodded. "If only."

"I will ask." He shrugged. 'Might take a while to get an answer."

"Fast as possible, huh? Some folk are close to running out of patience."

Swift winked. "I can understand that. Fast as possible." He sighed. "There are times when I really wonder how dumb people can get."

"Greed overrides good sense."

Swift laughed. "It is often a fatal disease."

A Very Mountainous Region.

The village, such as it was, was a small cluster of one story buildings, mainly dwellings, scattered along the narrow road.

Not far from the structures, the mountain slopes rose steeply to high peaks often capped by clouds.

This place felt to him as if the mountains had cracked apart millions of years ago and created this valley.

It was hard to imagine how this tiny settlement survived.

But they had and here he was.

Daniel had paid for lodgings for a week in one of the two rooms in the tiny inn, if that is what it was.

It appeared that the central room was the local gathering spot for whatever social activities the inhabitants engaged in.

And every night they gathered together here. First they seemed to just sit and watch him eat his meals. But, after two days, one, then another, came over to sit and hold small conversations with him. Their knowledge of English was good enough that he could follow most of what they said and they could follow what he said.

Now, having paid for another week's lodgings, he found that it was a very, very rare thing for them to have a visitor, of any kind. But they did have visitors, every year or so.

Now, they were discussing the tale of The Forest Ghost that Daniel had heard. Everyone agreed that it was not just a story but that such a thing really existed, out there in the forest.

All those that claimed that they had seen this thing indicated the same direction. And told him that the trail up that mountain side was steep and rough but that is where, high, high, high, The Forest Ghost lived.

No-one could give a good description of it as it was always seen just from the corner of a eye, a fleeting shadow shape, soft and silent as night itself. Yet, all agreed, it was not quite as tall as any of the villagers.

And so, three days later, Daniel started up the trail, small pack loaded with food and water, thick walking staff in one hand. He told them he would return late in the day.

Daniel wasn't worried. In his hands the staff was a lethal weapon.

The small group from the inn watched him slowly climb higher and disappear into the thick woods. Daniel didn't notice, nor could he have noticed, the eyes watching him. The villagers wondered to each other whether he would actually return. The Forest Ghost might not like strangers from outside the village.

A Market Town.

It had always been a market town as far back as the local population knew, and their history stretched back for hundreds of years. At first it was merely a few buildings at the crossroads.

But, then, the local population found that selling to those folks going from way over there to somewhere else was a good thing to do. The few farms brought produce to the crossroads and then as these things tend to do, the settlement grew as did the market.

Now the town was a rather moderate size in a region of mainly small villages. The town had a large central square around which the town stood, mostly stone structures, some dating from the almost beginnings of the town.

The market now occupied a goodly portion of the central square where throngs milled about and wandered from booth to booth.

Here and there at the edge of the square there were cafes. They all had numbers of tables set around their fronts where folk could sit, eat, drink, hold conversations, and watch the activity in the market.

At one of these tables, set off to one side and rather private, sat a short, heavy-set man wearing nondescript clothing.

Another man approached, pulled out a chair and sat.

"Hello, Donato," he said.

"Leo," said the other, filling two glasses with a deep red wine, locally produced, and pushing one across the small table.

Neither "Leo" nor "Donato" were their real names. Given the business, or businesses, they were in, it was prudent to keep one's actual identity unknown. But both of them maintained the fiction. It was good for business.

Leo took a swallow from his glass and smacked his lips. "A good year." He smiled.

Donato nodded. "Soooo?"

"A friend," began Leo. "An overseas friend asked a favor."

"A favor?"

"Uh huh."

"So?"

"This friend is not one that one would like to disappoint."

"Ah." Donato took a sip from his glass. Then he refilled both glasses.

Leo pulled a folded piece of paper from his inside coat pocket and set it on the table. Then he pulled an envelope from a side pocket. It was a very thick envelope. He set it on top of the paper and slid both across the table.

"My overseas friend would be very appreciative if you could help in the matter described on that paper."

Donato picked up the envelope, examined the contents, shoved it into the inner coat pocket, and opened the letter, and began to read, slowly.

Then he stared across the table. And licked his lips.

Leo nodded.

"This will take some time, not much, not little, just some."

Leo nodded. He emptied his glass. "I'll see you in a few days, same time, same place." He slid another piece of paper across the table, turned and strolled casually away.

Donato reread the letter again. This was going to take a very careful approach. But he knew just the pair that could find what was wanted. And knew that it was best if no-one knew why they were doing what they were doing.

So, he relaxed, watched the market activity, and finished

his wine.

A Very Mountainous Region.

He had climbed a considerable way up the mountain slope and walked into an almost flat area. The path wandered upward from this spot through the thick brush and into the thick woods hiding the mountain flank.

Wiping the sweat from his face, Daniel sat on a very handy, very large rock, and dumped his pack on the ground at his feet, leaning his walking staff again the rock.

Where he lived the elevation was not all that far above sea level, give or take some. In spite of having spent a number of days down in that small place, he was not really acclimated to this elevation.

He bent over, took out one of his water containers and took a drink. Something moved in that brush. He caught the movement from the corner of his eye. When he looked that way, he didn't see anything at all. He smiled to himself. So, there was something up here after all. It was just as he had been told. Then he took a folded map from his pack and opened it. There were a number of areas circled in red. That was the next thing to investigate. He had accumulated a number of reports and comments that related to a rather new gang of thugs/robbers/mercenaries that had operated in those areas. From what little he had learned, this mob had taken some ancient historic figure as their founding idol. It would be interesting to see how much of all that was real and how much was folk tale.

He sat and waited, patient as patient can be, wondering whether there was any reality here or just folk tale. He refolded the map and stuffed it back into his pack.

Nothing moved. Nothing made noise of any sort.

The Forest Ghost was a very cautious something.

Well, he thought, onward and upward. Perhaps that will bring it closer.

He stood, shrugged on his pack, grabbed his staff, and started along the barely visible trail.

She stepped silently from shadow and stared at him.

He stopped, stood absolutely still, and stared back. At a female, dressed all in black, a full head shorter than he was. Not exactly what he had thought a Forest Ghost would look like.

"My name is Daniel," he said gently. "Do you know this area?"

She watched his face, apparently unconcerned by his presence.

"Why are you here?" she asked, taking a step back.

"I heard a tale about a Forest Ghost and thought to see if there was anything to it." He pointed toward the valley floor. "The folk down there told me that such a thing existed. So, I decided to take a hike up this way just to see if it was true."

He thought that she had a nice voice, definitely not ghostly. So, she was an alive person who must live up here somewhere.

"Do you know anything about a Forest Ghost that lives up here?"

She shook her head. "People often have tales and beliefs and mythologies that they think are reality. It is their problem."

He nodded.

She took a sideways step and vanished.

Daniel hurried to where she had stood and looked. The trail ran parallel to the slope and into the forest. O.K., he thought, so that is the way to go. It seemed that the Forest Ghost had some reality after all. It was just a rather shy and retiring woman who managed to survive way up here.

He shrugged. And started along the trail, slowly,

cautiously.

He walked out into a rather open area, watching the trail very carefully. It was barely visible. The trail had been wandering for some time slightly higher but now was, more or less, on a level.

Suddenly he was hit from behind and crashed onto his face on the trail. Then he heard the loud bang.

Damn, he thought, I have been shot.

Darkness swallowed him as his senses faded away.

Washington, D.C.

Timothy Grimble strode down the hall humming a contented song to himself. It was a good day, this day, even this early in the day. It was one of several good days in a row. Things were going as planned. Today he wore a green tie with blue stars on it.

Swinging the door wide, he stepped into his offices. His secretary, as always there before he arrived, smiled at him, stood and handed him a stack of messages, and a number of envelopes still unopened.

He took them, smiled back, poured himself a cup of coffee, a morning ritual for him, and entered his space, a large room with windows along one side framing a view of sun-drenched neatly mown grass. And the city beyond.

Stepping behind his desk, he sat and swivelled around to face the window, took a sip from his cup, leaned forward and set the cup on the window sill, and began to read the messages, dropping them, one by one, into the paper shredder.

Taking another sip from his cup and returning it to its place on the sill, he began to open the envelopes, ripping the flap with one finger. He carefully read each one and then added them to the others in the shredder.

Holding his cup in one hand, he leaned back, both feet on the window sill.

And thought to himself, ah well, even though none of those messages had told what he wanted to know, none of them had been the bearer of bad news either.

He took another swallow from his cup and smiled to himself. Yep, things were going just as he had planned.

Swinging round he popped open a special mail account and sent a carefully worded message. Time to increase the amount of anxiety. Time to let that simmer for a few days, more or less, then he could make his first, out in the open, move.

Massachusetts.

Swift Nicky Tanagal looked at the large man sitting in the large chair on the other side of his desk.

Swift's eyes watched the other's face.

"What do you have?" asked Charles.

Swift leaned back, picked up one of the several phones on his desk and spoke to whoever was on the other end, hung up, and waited.

A burly man silently walked in, set a file on Swift's desk, and left, gently closing the door behind himself.

Swift opened it and took a quick glance at the paper

"O.K., we are looking at two matters."

Charles nodded.

"On the first matter some people, ah, friends, are slowly following a very twisted trail through a number of places in Europe." He frowned. "So far, a few folk seem to have died." He shrugged. "Guess they were not being helpful to the ones doing the searching."

His eyes stared into Charles' eyes. "Sorry. It is taking more time that I thought that it would."

Charles nodded, and sighed. "But progress is being made, right?"

"Yes. But on the second matter it appears events are happening in an unexpected way."

"Oh?"

Swift nodded and smiled. "I had someone carefully following Daniel Fanzle, as he calls himself, here and there, as you requested."

"And?"

"He was visiting a rather small cluster of homes in a deep valley in a rather isolated section, apparently asking the local folk about one of their favorite tales. Seems that he was interested in something they called The Forest Ghost. No-one has any idea as to why. We do know that he has been involved with a group trying to find a group of people from which the vampire and werewolf stories came. They think that there is a group out there who have behaviors that are responsible for the stories." He waved one hand in the air. "Daniel's associates do not believe in transformation and all that sort of thing, just that these folk do things that caused such stories to be generated."

Swift leaned back in his chair. "Paraphrasing that old song, Daniel went up the mountain and didn't come down again. The local folk told my man that Daniel took a hike up a trail that the locals said was the place where they had caught glimpses of the Forest Ghost. He had a backpack of food and water and a great thick hiking staff. They haven't seen him since. It has been a few days. Now all the locals won't go up that trail. Some of them are worried that his presence up there might bring the Forest Ghost down to terrorize their community."

Charles shook his head. "Wonder what happened to him. He is known to be quite capable of taking care of himself."

Swift shrugged.

Washington, D.C.

Charles and Randy met in Randy's company cafeteria.

It looked like a standard cafeteria. Overhead there were bright florescent lights. The floor was covered with non-ceramic tile of some sort in alternating blue and grey squares. The walls were painted soft yellow. All the tables were small, with dark brown tops, surrounded by four chairs. The serving area was the usual stainless steel with a slid-your-tray-along rails in front.

But the food was different. It was why Charles preferred to meet Randy here for lunch. The selection ranged from Italian to Chinese to Thai and things in between. The several chefs had been lured away from some of the best restaurants in the area, after proper vetting, of course.

Today Charles had, once again, taken the Thai dish, telling the server that 4 on the scale of heat 1-5, with 5 being the hottest, would be just fine.

Randy, as he often did, had a great leafy salad of some sort with a number of additional ingredients added to it.

Charles chewed, swallowed, and puffed air through his mouth. "Great food!" He took a swallow of his beverage from his large glass. The beverage was dark brown with a thick creamy head. One could get just about anything in beverages as well.

He looked across the table at Randy. "O.K., what's up?"

"Rasto Hardy has managed to hide himself pretty well. So we have started a search through everyone's name that we have in his organization, starting at the top, just as I said that we would. We are looking at bank transfers, building permits, land and real estate sales, things like that. We think that one of his troop might be hiding him in some place or another that is not directly connected to his enterprise or enterprises. What I mentioned before."

"Take much longer?"

"Depends. Two of my best are doing the research." He grinned. "We have a crack team ready to hit every place that pops up." He took another mouthful of his salad and chewed.

"No warning?"

"Nope." He nodded. "Just bust down the door and go in. And worry about it afterwards. If we get him, no-one will say anything."

Charles laughed. "Like I said before, that sounds like a plan, one of mine."

The Dusky Woods.

His eyes slowly opened and gradually focused.

Well, he thought, I am alive. Much better than the alternative. But where am I?

He tried to sit up and found that he was too weak to do that. So he turned his head, slowly he turned his head and stared at what he could see.

It was a rather plain room, one door, no window, some sort of a globe cast soft light around the room. One chest, and the bed he was lying in. The walls were soft brown wood in vertical slabs, the ceiling was grey rock roughly finished

Slowly, ever so carefully, he slid his hand up to the thick bandages covering his left shoulder. Moving that side was much too painful an idea.

He heard a soft sound, and turned his head that way.

She stood there and looked down at him. And nodded.

"I will bring you something to eat." She spun and left the room.

So, he lay there and stared at the ceiling.

She returned, set a tray on the chest and gently raised him to a sitting position, stuffing large pillows behind his back. And fed him, carefully cutting everything into small bites.

"This is very good," he said. He waggled his right hand at the room. "Many thanks for the care. What happened?"

"One of those dwellers from down below doesn't like you. A very not nice one."

He nodded and chewed. "Guess so."

She poked another mouthful in. "You will heal fast. Now."

He chewed and swallowed. "Thanks again. My name is Daniel Fanzle. May I know my savior's name? I assume that you are the one."

"Here is Dark Sibyl." She stood and yanked all the pillows away. "Now you will sleep." She spun and left the room.

He gasped as he thudded back. And fell asleep.

A Dense Forest.

Hofga was wandering aimlessly here and there some distance from his House. It was something that he did from time to time. As he walked along he wasn't worried about being injured by any of the local wildlife. Nothing that lived around here was a threat to him. Most things anywhere weren't.

So he strolled along, stopping now and then to admire a flower or a shrub, even a tree or two.

He enjoyed the solitude and the lack of company. Every once in awhile he felt the need to be alone, it was required. But only now and then, he grumbled silently to himself as he pondered over this or that. That was also required. Grumbling silently to himself. Pondering this or that.

Off to one side he saw a brighter patch of light in this dense forest. Must be a meadow, he thought, and headed that way.

Stepping out into the small grassy patch, he sat on a fallen tree and watched the birds and the butterflies going about their business.

Then it saw it. It coasted down into the meadow from somewhere high above. It looked like a bat turned into a bird, more or less. It was a soft green. The thing settled on a nearby tree limb and peered at him with bright blue eyes.

"What do you want?" he rumbled at it. It was a messenger from a House that he knew.

It told him.

"Ah dota!"

House Darthar.

The structure flowed in graceful curves around the great meadow set deep in a dense forest. At times it seemed as if the structure was actually part of the forest itself.

Hofga stomped across the meadow, heavy footsteps sending shock waves across the dense grass cover, and thumped upon the outside door.

The door swung open.

She stood in the opening and looked out at him. And laughed at his glower.

"Do come in, Hofga."

"Nothing to laugh about, Karanly, First Sister," he grumbled as he followed her down the hall and into a small room.

She walked to a counter and filled three cups with coffee and handed him one.

"Here, brother." She handed over another, took the last, sat down, and took a sip.

Othara, the House Head, sat, took a sip, and looked at Hofga.

"Ah, ummmmm."

"Darker frown than usual," suggested Karanly to Hofga.

Hofga took a sip.

"Ah dota," he grumbled.

"Ah um." Othara took a sip. "Sounds bad."

"House Arilia has a problem and wishes me to visit. They sent a messenger to me."

Orthara looked at Karanly. She shrugged.

"It is a small House," explained Hofga. "And a very secret one. A very, very secret one!" He took a sip. "Long ago I helped them with a small problem, a little."

"And the problem now?"

Hofga shrugged and took a sip. "The messenger did not explain what it was." He took another sip. "Ahhhhhh."

"Ummmmm."

"House Arilia uses two names for themselves."

Karanly took a sip. "Most, umm, strange."

Hofga held out his cup. She refilled it. "They are a secret House," he repeated.

He took a sip. "They have little to do with any of the other houses, as little as is possible." He stood. "I can tell you how to go."

Othara set his cup on a table. "Let's go outside."

Karanly walked to the outside door with them. "Tell me about the problem when you return."

Rugged and Isolated.

Batu had handled the financial matters of the group with an iron control. Now they stood and stared upward at their home away from home.

While members of the group could return to visit their home villages the process was carefully managed and designed to never call attention to that area. One by one, widely spaced in time, they returned to visit, to leave a small amount of financial support. This support was deliberately calculated to make life just that little bit of improvement that was possible for folk living in such isolation but never beyond that. The three villages understood and accepted that. They understood and accepted because they were proud of the activities of their sons and the care they took to keep harm far away.

So, now, they stood and stared upward at their home away from home.

It was an imposing sight. It had taken looking at and rejecting many sites that, at first glance, appeared to offer that which they sought. But, now, they had found it.

In a region of rugged terrain they had found and bought it. It was an up thrusting conical hill, more than a hill, less than a mountain, standing by itself. A narrow path crawled in a spiral up the steep slope to the summit where the real prize sat.

An ancient stone structure encased the top. It had obviously been placed to watch over the surrounding land. Batu had inspected it and found, much to his surprise, that they could easily repair the roofs and in a relatively short time bring the place up to minimal standards, sufficient to suit their needs.

After all, the three villages were they had been raised lived with minimal standards. And all members of the group had spent years walking and running up and down the mountainous slopes around the three villages.

So, they began.

Washington, D.C.

It was not a small office, it was not a large office, it was a comfortable office.

Charles leaned back in his chair, admired the landscape painting on one wall, and looked across his desk at his visitor.

He took a swallow from his coffee mug. "Pretty early in the morning, Randy."

Randy nodded and filled his cup from the carafe, and took a careful sip of the hot beverage. He was never sure what kind of coffee Charles might be having on any given morning. This was a good one.

"A number of my teams are about to visit a number of Rasto's high level troop's homes. I thought maybe if he started having folks get irritated at that level, folks complaining loudly, he might pop up, somewhere."

Charles laughed. "I like it."

"We are still searching land deeds and things like that."

Michigan.

Rondak opened the front door and walked in, arms loaded with grocery bags. He set them on the kitchen table and walked back outside for the rest of the supplies in the back seat of his car.

When he returned, Rasto was putting things in cabinets and the refrigerator.

"Made some phone calls when I was in town," Rondak said. "Not to worry, perfectly safe."

He filled a mug from the pot on the stove and sat at the kitchen table. "It is not good out there."

Rasto joined him. "Why?"

"They are systematically breaking down the doors of the houses and the business places of our personnel and causing lots of damage and leaving the same message."

Rasto stared at him. "Message?"

"Uh huh. They want you to talk with them. In person."

"Who? Are they?"

Rondak leaned forward and told him.

Rasto slumped in his chair. "Not good, not good at all."

"It can only get worse. They promised no stopping until everyone has had a visit. No far no-one has been hauled away, or locked up. Yet!"

"And what about us, did the message say?"

Rondak took a sip. "Not exactly."

"What does that mean?"

Rondak shrugged. "I have a hunch."

"Tell me, this hunch." Rasto straightened up and leaned toward his long-time friend.

Rondak told him.

House Darthar Na.

Jonathan stood on the bare rock of the narrow outcrop high on the mountain side and looked up.

White clumps of cloud drifted slowly across the mountain ridge gently scrapping their bottoms on the snow capped jagged rock. Now and then there was a clear patch of blue sky visible through the openings between the clouds

He could see them, high above the cloud layer, coasting in large circles, great wings extended, four pair of black wings and one pair of bright white. The fliers swooped and soared and sailed past each other. The group was obviously having a very good time. "Looks like fun," he observed.

"Ah dota!" agreed Hofga.

"Come down, Dee," he said. Jonathan spoke in a normal tone of voice, but he knew they could all hear him. It was a House Darthar skill. "We need to talk."

He watched them.

All the wings folded in as they plummeted down, a near vertical predator's dive. Then he lost sight of them as clouds drifted between them.

Suddenly they appeared, hurtling from the bottom of the cloud layer. Wings snapped to full extension. They swooped up and over his head, circled around, and coasted gently to a landing nearby.

Daliera and her two daughters, Tiela and Winala, looked puzzled at their visitors. The two Tarken, gigantic eagle-like birds, merely watched.

"What brings the Head of House Darthar up here?" asked Dee. "Lord Othara?" She laughed at his expression. "Hi, Hofga."

Jonthan sighed, quietly to himself. Her people upbringing seemed to bubble up at peculiar times.

"We need to visit House Arilia, you, me, and Hofga."

"House Arilia?"

"It is a very, very secret house," explained Hofga.

"Isn't it dangerous to just pop up on one of those?"

Jonathan smiled. "Hofga knows them."

"Oh, all right." She looked over. "Daughters, take the Tarken to the house. We can talk later." Her white wings disappeared as daughters and Tarken took to the air. Wings were a House Darthar Na skill.

She looked at Jonathon. "My House first. I need to change clothes."

He nodded.

Vermont.

Ziaza Sowden was lounging in her pajamas, in the early morning light, on her rear deck, sipping coffee and watching the birds jump about.

She considered this the very best part of any day, especially on a summer day. Quiet and comfortable.

Her phone rang, interrupting the quiet.

She picked it up, looked at the display, and laughed.

The display read: "Good Morning, Ms. Phelps, we have a mission, if you choose to take it." It was the second time that he had used that display.

"Hi, Charles, what do you want? Pretty early in the day for this."

He laughed. "Washington, D.C., the city that never sleeps, so to speak. You and your's doing anything?"

"No. Everyone is on a little R'n'R. It keeps then alert when we are working."

"Got a big bucks job for you, Ziaza."

"Another? Doing?"

"It is time to start watching Timothy Grimble big time. We have folk doing this and that but I would like you and your group to do that as well." He laughed loudly. "Of course, Ms. Phelps, if you are caught we will deny all knowledge of you."

She grinned. "What's up, Charles?"

"Sneaky Tim will soon find out that he is not very sneaky or smart. We need to pile up as much knowledge about his behavior as we can get. Your guys are very good at watching and documenting stuff like that there."

"O.K. When do we have to start?"

"ASAP!"

"Sure. We can begin tomorrow morning. Fast enough?"

"KA-CHING!"

She laughed again. She did like talking with him. "Thanks, Charles."

"I just hope all the money that you all are making doesn't mean that there are plans in your future to retire."

"I'll let you know. If!"

"Sounds good to me. Ahhhhhhhh."

"What?"

"Thanks, Ziaza."

She was so startled that she couldn't think of a reply before he hung up.

She disconnected, then dialed two numbers, one after the

other, and left the same message. And slumped in her chair. Her crews would be very busy for the rest of the day, reaching out, finding more capable folk to make the effort as large as possible and yet remain manageable.

She leaned back in her chair and enjoyed the rest of the early morning and sipped her coffee. And watched the birds jump around.

The next day she added a few additional items to her ready pack, snatched it up and walked into the garage.

As she passed down the narrow road and one of her neighbors, she waved and honked her horn three times.

He waved back, and would watch her place until she returned. They swapped favors.

It was a very rural area after all.

House Darthar Na.

They stood in the meadow that stretched upwards from the surrounding forest in a gentle slope to the base of the many storied structure to the base of the entry stairs. The house was half chateau, half fairytale castle. Everything was constructed of light red wood perched on heavy dark green stone foundation walls, roofs of soft brown. The whole thing stretched along the slope rather than up and down the mountain's flank.

Janice stood at the top of the stairs. She had just knocked on the outer door, and was waiting patiently.

Dee walked up the stairs and pushed the door open. "Do come in, all."

As the group walked down the hall paneled in golden oak, paintings hung everywhere, she looked over. "So, Janice?"

Dee turned them into an appropriate sized room, served them coffee, and stepped to the open door. "Be back in a bit. Need a shower."

Janice, Hofga, and Jonathan sat and sipped at their coffee.

Jonathan looked over the rim of his cup at her. "Ah ummm."

She took a sip. "Wait for Dee."

He nodded.

Hofga stood and refilled their cups.

And after a not too long wait, Dee returned. She picked up a cup, sat, took a sip, and looked at her friend and long-time associate.

Janice carefully explained what she had found during her research about the company and the individual looking into certain areas of the People mythology.

A Very Mountainous Region.

The four of them stood far up the mountain in an almost flat area. The path wandered from the thick brush, through this almost flat area, and into the thick woods hiding the mountain flank.

There was a small cave in the mountain side, more a deep indentation than cave.

Hofga stepped into the shallow space and gently thumped on a large rock. And waited, as patient as he could be. For him that meant shifting his weight from foot to foot and mumbling softly.

A section of the rock face shifted and opened inward. She looked out, all blank face.

Hofga waggled his hand at the others. "Here is Othara, Head of House Darthar. He prefers to be called Jonathan. Here is Daliera of The Fontala, Head of House Darthar Na. Here is Janice, Third Daughter of House Hinterane. All come to visit." He scuffed one boot in the small amount of dirt. "I asked them."

She nodded at him and looked at the others. "Here is Dark

Sibyl, House Head. Do come in, all. Welcome to House Arilia, The Dusky Woods."

She led them down a tunnel carved from the mountain and into a small room. Turning to a large table, she filled cups and handed them around, and waved at the chairs, and sat.

After all had settled and taken a sip or two, she said, "I asked Hofga to come because we have some small problem and felt that he might be able to suggest a solution. Apparently he felt that others ought to be involved. House Arilia trusts Hofga more than most. If he believes this is so, then we have no feeling of not nice in this matter."

She stood and refilled their cups, then her own, and sat, and took a sip.

"House Arilia is a secret house. We do not involve ourselves in most matters of our folk, nor do we wish to have others involved in our matters." She took a sip, her eyes dancing from face to face.

"However, we now have a small problem, we, I, am responsible for, and wish more, ummmmm, experienced folk, like Hofga, to speak with us on this matter."

"Ah dota!" Hofga emptied his cup.

Threads

House Arilia.

Dark Sybil looked from face to face. And took a sip from her cup.

"We rarely have visitors so I may be somewhat, ummmmm, not polite."

Jonathon nodded. "Of little concern."

Hofga took a sip and shrugged. "Problem?" he reminded her.

She stood and refilled all the cups and returned to her seat.

"We have a House skill. The people find it hard to see us." She took a sip. "A unknown one of the People was seen visiting that small cluster of People down below. That male appeared to be doing nothing but visiting and talking with them. It was curious, not the usual visitor activity, so I went below to see. That one was most interested in talking with them about their mythological belief in what they called The Forest Ghost. Most unusual. Visitors infrequently come to this isolated place. One or two every several years, as the People measure time. But none were ever interested in local superstitions like that." She took a sip. "They usually just smile politely at being told that tale. None ever seem to take it seriously. That one did take it serious."

"Another House skill is that we are able to, ah ummm, feel the reality of the People if we are close enough. That male is quite unique. His mind works quick quick. He seems to see connections others do not."

She looked from face to face. And took a sip and checked that their cups still were full enough.

"After two weeks, as the People measure time, we saw that one start up the trail that leads high into the mountains on this side the valley. It was obvious that male must dwell at much lower heights." She smiled. "He was breathing quite hard and loud."

"We met that one for just an instance on a lower spot. He asked me if I was The Forest Ghost." Her smile broadened. "I told him that it was merely people mythology and stepped behind the thick shrubbery."

"Much to my surprise that one continued up the trail and even higher. While that one was walking along a mostly flat stretch one of those bottom dwellers fired a People weapon at him and ran off." She took a sip. "A very not nice bottom dweller," she grumbled.

"I inspected the body and found small signs of life. I brought him here and we did fast healing. He now sleeps until we bring him awake." She shrugged, and took a sip.

"This is the problem." She frowned at something only she could see. "Fast healing will leave a small Feyra trace behind. For any of us this is no problem. For one of The People we have no idea. But that male of the People will have some small sense of The Feyra. What do we do with that one?"

"Ah dota!" gasped Hofga.

Dark Sybil laughed. And refilled his cup.

Jonathan took a sip. "Daliera was raised as one of the People."

Dark Sybil stared at her. "Word did come to us of that. We found it hard to accept."

"My parents were trying to protect me from some very not nice ones. No longer a problem for me." Dee took a sip. "How will this small sense of us express itself with that one?"

"Ummmmmm. I believe that given that one's unusual

mental process that it may be expressed as a feeling that we are what we are, if that one does meet one of us somewhere."

Dee took a sip. And looked at Jonathon. "Not very likely that he would."

Jonathon nodded.

Dark Sybil took a sip. "He told me his name so we will always be able to find that one. If there is ever need."

"And it is?" asked Dee.

"That one calls himself Daniel Fanzle at the moment. I could see that it was not his only name."

Janice jerked. "True?"

"Most so," said Dark Sybil, staring at the expression on Janice's face.

"Janice?" Dee took a sip.

Janice sat back in her chair. "As I told you." She looked at Dark Sybil. "I did some research asked for by the House Head. My father deals in old documents, as the People measure time, that speak of their mythological beliefs, what they call fairy tales, creation stories, and the other nonsense things that they believe. He received a request for materials about werewolves, vampires, and angels. As the House Head had never heard of that one of the People before, I was asked to do research. Based on that, the House Head decided to ignore the request." She took a sip. "You have that one here, in your House. The House Head felt that the one making the request might be not nice. Past requests of a similar nature have been attempts to, ah um, interfere."

"Prata!" Hofga held out his just emptied cup. "If that one sleeps long long it will no longer be a problem."

Dark Sybil shook her head. "I do not heal just to kill!" She refilled his cup.

"Ahhhhhhh ummmmmm." Hofga took a sip.

Jonathon looked over. "Dee?"

Dee nodded. "Just put him down below and let him wake. This Daniel will be healed but have no idea of who or how. It will be a puzzle. If he comes back up here will he be able to find the House?"

Dark Sybil shook her head. "This is a very secret house. Most Feyra could not." She smiled. "Hofga is one of the very few who can do that."

Jonathon looked from face to face, stood and bowed to her. "Dee, Jancie, and I will leave. Hofga, it appears, wishes to visit some."

Dark Sybil led them to the outside door and touched each of them on a shoulder. "Do come again."

Massachusetts.

It was one of the older but well maintained houses. It was perched on a high spot near the shore. As Charles climbed from his truck, he could see a number of large men wearing windbreakers wandering here and there around the building. It was perfectly normal for this place.

Inside the large living room sat Swift Nicky Tanagal, lounging in a chair, dressed in very casual attire that reeked of money. He smiled at Charles and waggled one hand at the empty chair. "Please sit."

Charles sat, slumped comfortably, and took a swallow of the beverage handed to him by one of the men. All the large men wearing wind breakers wandered from the room closing the door after them.

A very large man, large, mostly muscle, little fat, sat in the other chair, glass of red wine in one hand, a deep glower on his face.

"Charles," said Swift, "meet Rasto Hardy."
Charles nodded.

"Rasto is very unhappy," explained Swift Nicky. "But I do believe he is willing to talk with you, with us." Swift took a swallow from his glass. "Cognac, very old."

Charles laughed, a very happy laugh, and looked at Rasto. "Good to hear. The talking part." He took another swallow from his mug.

He nodded at Rasto. "Sooooo?"

"Mr. Tanagal said that you were willing to listen." Rasto cleared his throat. "And stop, eh, doing things."

Charles nodded again. "We might do that. Depending."

"Upon what?" snapped Rasto.

"Upon what you wish to tell us."

"Like?"

"Rasto, everyone knows that you are very good at making people disappear, alive."

"And?"

"We know you took a bunch of money from Harold Tridler." Charles handed Rasto a number of photographs. "Nice shots, don't you think?"

"O.K., so I did." Rasto took a big swallow from his glass.

Swift stood and leaned over his desk, a wine bottle in one hand. "More?"

"Sure!"

Swift refilled Rasto's glass.

Charles took a sip from his mug. "All I want to know is who the person you snatched was handed to, nothing else."

Rasto nodded. "O.K. And you will ease up?" He took a big swallow from his glass.

"You betcha. Who?"

Rasto leaned toward Charles. "I only know the one name. He is the beginning of the chain, so to speak."

"Good enough." Charles sat back. "Who?"

"Our secret that I told you?"

"Absolutely."

Rasto took a pen and paper from inside his jacket, leaned on the desk, wrote something, and handed it to Charles. "May I go now?"

Swift waggled a hand at him. "Bye, Rasto."

Rasto lurched to his feet, set his glass on a table, and banged out the door. "Let's go, Rondak!"

Charles sighed. "Certainly hope this is good information. Powerful people are getting impatient."

Swift held out a hand. "I will get it checked."

Charles handed him the piece of paper. "Thanks, buddy." He stood and strolled toward the door. "See ya."

Swift Nicky laughed. "Always a pleasure, Charles."

Virginia.

His eyes wobbled open and slowly focused on the ceiling. It looked familiar that ceiling and that didn't make a whole lot of sense. How did he get here from there, way up the side of that mountain lying on his face and, apparently, dying. He frowned. For a moment he had a vague sense of something else.

Daniel Fanzle slowly sat up, much to his surprise that he could do that. He didn't feel any pain at all and there ought to be lots and lots of that. He opened his pajama top and slid careful hands over where he knew there ought to be damage. Smooth, unblemished skin with just a tiny pucker mark.

He looked around the room. That's why he recognized the ceiling. He was in his bedroom in his home, thousands of miles from where he had been last, lying on his face in the dirt, with no idea of how he came to be where he was now or how he came to be so healed and healthy.

Swinging his legs around, he stood. And laughed. Now

here was a mystery to solve, he thought.

His clothes were neatly folded on one of the chairs. So he walked over and dressed. As he did so, he noted a small, folded note sitting on the table.

After tying his shoe laces, he stood, walked over, picked it up, opened it and read it.

Daniel Fanzle.

Good health.

Dark Sybil.

Daniel smiled broadly, now he remembered the one time only, and wondered how she did whatever she did. He felt really good. How she managed to get him home, put him inside his own bedroom, was beyond thinking about.

He walked from the room, down the stairs and into the kitchen to make something to eat. Looking out the window he could see that it was morning, well maybe mid-morning. Checking the kitchen clock he saw that it was so.

Taking things from the refrigerator, he made a very large breakfast. He was quite hungry. Must be from all that healing he had to have done.

As he sat, drinking coffee and scooping up the last of the egg yoke with the last bit of toast, Hank Schmidt walked in.

"Welcome home," he said. "Good trip?"

Daniel smiled. "Indeed. A very interesting trip." Yep, he thought, no-one knew that he had been brought home in some unknown way by some unknown people, some very clever people.

Hank handed him a stack of envelopes. "Lots of stuff piled

up in your absence."

Daniel took them, quickly sorted through them, and found one which he opened right away. "Now that is interesting." The Antiquarian Dealer in old documents wasn't interested in his business.

He stood. "I'll be in the library for some time, things to think about." Like how he had lost close to two weeks, he added to himself. And healed so quickly.

"I'll make a pot of coffee." Hank turned to start doing that as Daniel walked from the room, already wondering about the time period of which he had no remembrance.

A Market Town.

It had always been a market town as far back as the local population know, and their history stretched back for hundreds of years. At first it was merely a few buildings at the crossroads.

But, then, the local found that selling to those folks going from way over there to somewhere else was a good thing to do. The few farms brought produce to the crossroads and then as these things tend to do, the settlement grew as did the market.

Now the town was a rather moderate size in a region of mainly small villages. The town had a large central square around which the town stood, mostly stone structures, some dating from the almost beginnings of the town.

The market now occupied a goodly portion of the central square where throngs milled about and wandered from booth to booth.

Here and there at the edge of the square there were cafes. They all had numbers of tables set around their fronts where folk could sit, eat, drink, hold conversations, and watch the activity in the market.

At one of these tables, set off to one side and rather

private, sat a short heavy set man wearing nondescript clothing.

Another man approached, pulled out a chair and sat.

"Hello, Fritz," he said.

"Juan," said the other, filling two glasses with a deep red wine, locally produced, and pushing one across the small table.

Neither "Fritz" nor "Juan" were their real names, which both of them understood. Given the business, or businesses, they were in, it was prudent to keep one's actual identity unknown. But both of them maintained the fiction. It was good for business. The pair changed names as other folk changed shirts.

Juan took a swallow from his glass and smacked his lips. "Another good year." He smiled.

Fritz nodded. "Soooo?"

"A friend," began Juan. "An overseas friend asked for a favor. Again."

"A favor? Again?"

"Uh huh."

"So?"

"This friend is not one that one would like to disappoint."

"Ah." Fritz took a sip from his glass. Then he refilled both glasses. So, it was that same "friend."

Juan pushed a piece of paper across the table. "This time it will be better. I recognized this name. Do be very careful. He has a large, well financed organization." He reached over and set a very thick envelope on top of the paper.

Fritz shrugged. He wasn't bothered by either large, or well-financed, organizations.

"Information is required. My friend will send sufficient funds in addition."

Fritz nodded. "I'll let you know how things go." His was a small and rather well financed organization, and getting even more well financed, it seemed.

Washington, D.C.

Timothy Grimble hurried down the hall. It was turning out to not be a good day, this day, even this early in the day.

Swinging the door wide, he stepped into his offices. His secretary, as always there before he arrived, smiled at him, stood and handed him a stack of messages, and a number of envelopes still unopened.

He took them, smiled back, poured himself a cup of coffee, a morning ritual for him, and entered his space, a large room with windows along one side framing a view of sun-drenched neatly mown grass. And the city beyond.

Stepping behind his desk, he sat and swivelled around to face the window, took a sip from his cup, leaned forward and set the cup on the window sill, and began to quickly read through the messages, dropping them, one by one, into the paper shredder.

Taking another sip from his cup and returning it to its place on the sill he began to rip open the envelopes, viciously tearing the flaps to ragged shreds with one finger. He read each one and then added them to the others in the shredder.

Holding his cup in one hand, he leaned back, both feet on the window sill.

And thought to himself, things seemed to be getting too loose for his comfort, both here at home and elsewhere.

Staring out the window, he began to ponder whether he ought to abandon it, his great plan. He took a quick swallow from his cup. No, not yet. But he would begin to consider how to, ahhhhh, undo certain things he had caused to happen. He might need some insurance.

Taking a slim note pad from inside his jacket he began to thumb through the various entries and began to make a mental list of actions that could be brought into existence. If necessary.

Maryland.

They were just finishing dinner when someone knocked on their front door.

Charles stood. "I'll get it."

He strolled down the short hall and opened the front door.

"Hi," said Janice.

Charles smiled at them and stepped back. "Do come in. All." He had learned, from Ralph, that this was the proper thing to say to any of The Feyra waiting to enter a home. They couldn't, they were unable to, enter any Feyra dwelling without being asked to *do come in* and wouldn't enter any non-Feyra house either without being asked, most of the time. It was considered a breach of good manners to enter without being asked. He didn't know that no one, Feyra or one of the people, would be able to enter any Feyra house without be asked to enter by a family member. It was an aspect of the house structure itself. The Flaming Swords, the staff that The Fontala carried, could overwhelm that with ease, usually by cutting the door from the building.

Janice, Dee, and Purr Cat, a Furleen, a great feline, lion-sized, cougar-looking, all bronze fur with white tiger stripes on her shoulders and neck, walked in. Dee had named this Furleen, Purr Cat, when she was first getting used to the idea that she was one of The Feyra, and The Head of House Darthar Na, and was meeting all the house beasts, a unique aspect of House Darthar Na. A few of the Feyra Houses might have a single house beast of some sort. House Darthar Na had a number of rare species.

Prentice, Charles' wife, and Richlin, their college-age daughter smiled at them.

Purr Cat walked around the table and bumped Richlin with her head.

"Heya." Richlin scratched behind one fuzzy ear. She had

met the Furleen before.

Dee and Janice sat at the table and smiled at everyone.

Charles poured a cup of coffee for Dee and Janice. "We were just going to have dessert. Join us? We have plenty."

Dee sipped and nodded.

"Most kind," said Janice. She took a sip.

Prentice stood. "I'll bring it in." She hurried to the kitchen and wondered what was going on. She knew that The Feyra called themselves The Hidden Ones and wished to remain so. Yet Dee and the Furleen had, once again, just strolled into their house.

Dessert was a multi-layer vanilla strawberry cake with a side scoop of ice cream. Charles preferred chocolate ice cream but would eat whatever was served. Dee and Janice had vanilla ice cream. To The Feyra, chocolate was a horrid taste.

Charles smiled at Dee. "So, this is a surprise."

Dee smiled back. "I wish to know something."

Charles nodded, and wondered what was going on this time. "Sure. If I can. What?"

"Can you tell me anything about a male of the People who names himself Daniel Fanzle?"

Charles almost choked on his mouthful of cake, almost. He took a quick swallow of his beverage and stared at her.

"Ah ummmmm." Dee took a sip from her cup.

Charles lips twisted back and forth and then looked at Richlin. "Kiddo, go sit in your room for awhile. Please. Take your dessert with you."

When his daughter was well out of hearing, Richlin knew that much of what her parent's activities were not to be overheard, he frowned at Dee. "Information about that guy is so classified that I could get shot for telling anyone. But!" He smiled. "I'll tell you." And shrugged. "So who could ever know."

He leaned toward her and began to relate everything that he knew. It took quite awhile. By the time he was finished all had finished their dessert and sat there sipping from their cups, refilled twice by Prentice.

"Ah ummmm." Dee took a sip.

Charles took another slice of the cake and leaned back in his chair. "Soooooooooo, why do you want to know about him?" He cut off a piece and began to chew.

Dee took a sip from her cup. "He is a nice, ah, person?"

Charles did choke this time. He knew that *nice* and *not nice* in the Feyra language were terms that had much more meaning than in English. Ralph has told him that *not nice* encompassed the English terms, despicable, sleazy, perverted, dirty rotten mean, as well as most of the truly awful things that one could think of. He had been also told that The Feyra felt that not nice ones should have short lives.

Taking a big swallow from his glass, he cleared his throat, several times, and gasped, "YES! Daniel is actually quite a nice guy. In fact I would say that he is very nice."

Dee nodded and took a sip.

"Why?"

She stared into his eyes. "That male has become of, ah ummmm, interest to us. We were, ah ummm, concerned." She took a sip. "It is good to know that he is . . . nice."

Charles slumped in his chair and stared at her. What on earth had Daniel been up to that Dee came here just to ask those questions. He knew that the Feyra were very much concerned that they remain The Hidden Ones and well outside of the knowledge of the rest of us, whom they called The People. He also knew, from past events, that anyone that tried to interfere with them wound up very dead.

He smiled at her. "I don't think that you should have any

worries about Daniel. He may have a very high curiosity and a powerful intellect to go with it, but he would never deliberately bring harm to anyone." He shrugged. "Unless they deserved it." He laughed. "In fact, that guy really seems to get along with any group that he meets. Regardless of what they think or how they behave. As long as they keep to themselves."

Dee stood. "Great thanks, Charles." She nodded at Prentice. "Good dessert."

She headed for the outside door, followed by Janice and Purr Cat.

When he heard the door open and close, Charles sighed. "Oh boy."

Prentice reached over and set a hand on his hand. "Dear?"

"I am not sure. But I think that something that Daniel was doing came to her attention and that she wasn't sure what to do about that."

He patted her hand with his free one. "I think we just saved his life."

House Ritilar.

Nyecol was, once again, visiting the small settlement two miles down the dusty and rutted trail from where her house was located. That trail passed as a road in this very isolated region deep inside the great mountain range and stretched from here far down into an open plain. Her house specialized in making those implements that the local population used in their daily activities.

While she was trading, she noticed that a strange group of The People that had arrived in a great vehicle capable of driving this far were in a heavy debate with the inn keeper. The rather young woman that the inn keeper had received a great sum of money to guard was looking very disturbed. The strangers handed the inn keeper a thick bundle of the local people currency, climbed into their machine and rushed away.

The people really do strange, Nyeko thought, as she finished her small transactions and started back toward her house. She noted that the watch thing was still there, wrapped in dark shadow, watching the inn keeper's dwelling.

The Garden Tower.

It was a twelve story, square, apartment complex with a roof garden set in the middle of acres of well maintained grass. The wide open space was edged by the broad and dense belt of trees. It made this a very private place to live.

The parking structure for the residents was mostly underground with only the upper story above ground. Each of the very expensive apartment complexes had allocated to them three adjacent parking spots. Each spot wide enough that doors open on the vehicles at the same time in the adjacent slots could not hit each other nor block the passage of occupants.

A long tunnel led from the second level of the structure to the below ground mezzanine of the tower. This space and the tunnel, sides and ceiling, were paneled in wood with the floor covered in large tiles, colors that complimented the walls and ceiling. All lighting was indirect and plentiful. The tunnel and the mezzanine had pseudo-windows set here and there with three-dimensional scenery so no one might feel enclosed. It was a very pleasant stroll from the parking structure to the tower. The paintings that hung on the walls were changed the first of every month, late a night.

In the mezzanine there were a number of elevators labeled with the floors that they served. One had 1-3 on a panel above the doors, one had 3-6, one had 7-9, one had 10-11, and one had 12. Each elevator only opened with the appropriate swipe card. Every apartment complex had another card for the front door.

There was a button in each elevator for the ground floor where the elegant restaurant was located. The ground floor was served by a separate tunnel from a loading bay. All deliveries came this way and were taken by the staff to the appropriate apartment complex.

The entire project had been financed by a combination of funds: some very private, some from the primary contractor, and some from various public funds.

The top floor, with the roof garden, was occupied by a company whose name never appeared on any document. Here there were luxurious bedrooms and a very large living room, all having great outside windows offering a view of the open space surrounding the tower.

In the evening, year round, artfully placed lighting illuminated all the space from the base of the tower to the distant tree line.

All the residents on floors one to eleven thought that this was a very nice touch. It was very pleasant at night to watch local wildlife wandering about on all the neatly mown grass.

Those folk that utilized the top floor had other reasons for all that lighting which they did not share with the rest of the residents.

Virginia.

Daniel Fanzle was taking a stroll along the wheel ruts that passed as a secondary road not too far from his home. A slow stroll in a quiet environment was a good thing to do when he was puzzling over the number of different things that he had been interested in during the recent past, the more or less recent past.

So, as his mind drifted from one piece of information to another, he strolled along the tree shadowed sorta road.

Suddenly he jerked to a halt, his eyes flying wide open.

"HOLY COW!"

He lurched to one side and sat heavily onto a nearby fallen tree and stared at the ground. "Holy cow! They are real, really, really real!"

Then he looked up, seeing other things, other places, hearing other conversations, and smiled and laughed out loud.

That woman was The Forest Ghost, not some just-so story. She wasn't just some folk tale in an isolated valley bottom. Then the long ago story he had read about the hunter and the Spirit of The Woods that befriended him must be true as well. That hunter did meet an unknown group that lived somewhere other than among the people that the hunter knew. Daniel laughed out loud again.

"Amazing!" So that meant that Doma Sparta had really met an angel, after all.

He stared at the surrounding wood and began to wonder how many other folk were out there that folk tales and mythology had misinterpreted or pushed into some cultural never-never land.

His mind jittered with excitement. This was the most exciting thing he had ever bumped into.

Jumping to his feet, he hurried back toward his house, rapidly planning how to approach this problem. But, he would have to be very careful. After all, The Forest Ghost had somehow gotten him into his own bedroom without anyone knowing how or when as well as healing him in a remarkably short time.

And what do you do when you meet an angel? A real one?

Maryland.

Randy took a large bite from his sandwich and nodded at Ralph. They were eating in Ralph's home kitchen. "Pretty good." Randy was having a sandwich rather than his usual salad. This time.

Ralph did the same and agreed. He did make pretty good sandwiches.

Ralph took a sip from his orange juice. "I think that it is time we had a little talk with a certain lobbyist named Harold Tridler."

Randy to a swallow of his tea. "You sure?"

"Yep. And let's hope he will give us what we want."

Randy smiled. "Oh, I am sure that he will." He picked up his sandwich. "When?"

"Two days from now should be fine."

Randy nodded. "Plenty of time to set things up." He took another large bite from his sandwich.

Washington, D.C.

The phone on Charles' desk buzzed. He picked it up and punched the pulsating red button.

"What?"

He listened. And laughed.

"Send her right along."

He shoved all the papers on his desk top into a folder, stuffed the folder into the appropriate drawer, locked the drawer, leaned back in his chair, and watched the door to his office.

It was a few minutes walk to his office from the front desk.

And in a few minutes the door was opened by a tall man. "Go right in." He stepped back and waited.

The door opened. She strolled in, sat in a handy chair,

"Bit of a surprise." He smiled at her. "What's up?"

He took a sip from his cup of coffee, just black coffee, and looked at her, the very pretty woman who sat in one of the guest chairs. He thought, once again, that she had a rather exotic appearance. Black hair, light tan skin, high cheek bones, dark brown almost black somewhat oval eyes. She set a folder on his desk.

Setting his cup down, he pulled the folder over, opened it, read something, looked at her, and smiled.

"So I won't ask how you got all his e-mails."

"Grimble is dirty, through and through." She frowned darkly at the folder he held. "He is also someone that needs to be thumped mightily with a 2 x 4 or something else equally as hard and heavy."

Charles nodded. "Kidnapping is a nasty thing to do and tends to get people put away for a long, long time in unpleasant places."

"He appears to be a very slippery character."

Charles refilled her cup. "Not all that slippery as he thinks. We can't grab him yet. But we will. Thanks for all the work. Keep watching this guy. O.K.?"

She stood. "O.K." And headed for the door.

"Ka-ching!" he called at her back.

House Ritilar.

Nyecol was cautiously approaching the small settlement two miles down the dusty and rutted trail from where her house was located. The trail that passed as a road in this very isolated region deep inside the great mountain range.

She had been intending to do some trading, but she could see that another strange group of The People had arrived in a great vehicle capable of driving this far.

The inhabitants were greatly agitated and running in and out of their houses while a group of the new ones was engaged in a heavy debate with the inn keeper. The rather young woman that the inn keeper had received a great sum of money to guard was looking very frightened. It appeared that the People of the settlement were keeping these others from approaching her.

The strangers were waving their arms and yelling at the inn keeper and the rest of the population.

Nyecol stopped and slipped into the trees that lined the narrow trail to observe and remain hidden, her clothes blending into the surrounding vegetation.

Suddenly the strangers pulled strange people weapons from their backs and began shooting out windows in the surrounding structures. Four of them shoved the inn keeper to the side and grabbed the young woman who had screamed and tried to run away.

Shoving her into their great vehicle while the others continued to destroy the settlement's structures, they began yelling at the others, waving their arms as the great thing made roaring sounds.

The inhabitants began to run into the surroundings woods while others began to throw rocks and stones at the vehicle and the very angry People that had come in it.

The ones creating all the noise hurriedly ran to their People machine and continued to shoot at the structures as the great thing roared down the rutted trail, a great cloud of dust rising behind it as it banged down the narrow canyon and disappeared.

Nyecol slipped from her cover, turned, and ran for her house.

Virginia.

Daniel Fanzle sat at his desk, now covered with all the materials that he had gathered on all the mythologies. He was carefully reading each page searching for those bits and pieces that hadn't seemed all that important before.

He copied these bits and pieces on a note pad, and marked

notes and comments on the several large maps spread on the table he had pulled close to his desk.

He took time to eat lunch, give instructions to Hank to pass on to the rest of the staff, and worked on.

Late in the afternoon, he leaned back, and sighed. Not much for all that labor, he thought. But it was a good beginning, and a better focus.

Picking up one of the sheets, he reread those few things that he felt were factual.

They wore dark clothes. No-one seemed to have good idea of where they actually lived. He knew that at least one of them lived near where he had been hiking and that she, and he assumed, some others, had some interesting skills, both in terms of healing and the ability to sneak him into a country that was very concerned with not having people sneak into it. Not only that, they could get him inside his home without any of his staff knowing it. He felt that was a very interesting and a very high level skill.

From personal experience he knew that while they spoke his language they had a slight accent, which he could not place. And they had great self confidence, assuming he could project from the one to the many.

So, given what little he actually knew, what should he do?

Leaning back in his swivel chair, he stared out a window and thought. Then he laughed. Now there was an idea! He laughed again. Guess he would just have to go and surprise some people.

Washington, D.C.

Timothy Grimble reviewed, once again, his very carefully composed note to The President. He had spent most of the morning in his office, shut off from the outside world, editing and rewriting and editing again until he felt that this statements, a series of tightly worded paragraphs were absolutely clear and to the point. It contained scraps of various pieces of intelligence to bolster the presentation, all of which he normally had access to. He knew that all that was quite false. But it would be impossible to verify. He smiled. That was the best part of it.

Then he began to write out the final few paragraphs carefully arguing how he could bring to an end and a positive conclusion the very problem that The President had been so skillfully keeping hidden from the press and all the rest of his staff.

One more time he reread and changed a word here and a word there. Then he printed it out and wrote the whole thing by hand on the thick stationary embossed with his office letterhead. A hand-written message would have much greater impact, be much less bureaucratic.

Surprises

Maryland.

He stood on the front steps and knocked on the door and waited.

The house looked, more or less, like all the other houses in this area of moderately-sized, moderately priced houses.

The grass was neatly trimmed, the house was well maintained. All in all, it was just one house among all the others with neatly trimmed lawns and well maintained exteriors.

The door swung in and she looked out.

"Yes?"

"May I speak to Ralph, please?"

"Name?"

"Daniel Fanzle."

"Wait one."

She closed the door.

He waited.

Then the door opened. "Come in," she said, as she stepped back.

As he stepped inside and closed the door, she said, "This way. He is in the living room."

They walked down a short hall and entered the living room. The two men standing there looked at him. One was a rather large, football player looking guy. The other was shorter and rather compact. Neither face held any expression at all. They looked at him and waited.

The woman sat in a nearby chair.

"Yes?" said the smaller of the pair.

"Hello, Ralph. My name is Daniel Fanzle and I would like to talk to you about something."

The large one laughed. "I'm Charles. Take a seat." He dropped into the large couch and picked up a tall glass filled with amber liquid that had a thick white foam cap.

Ralph sat in a comfortable chair and pointed to another.

Daniel sat there.

"O.K.," said Ralph. "What?"

Daniel smiled. "As you probably know I have been involved with a group that is chasing certain mythologies believing that there are real folk behind those mythologies."

Ralph nodded.

Charles and Sandra watched Daniel.

He assumed that they were not as relaxed as they appeared to be. After all, where they lived was not supposed to be known to anyone.

Daniel took a deep breath. "Please don't laugh until I am done."

Ralph nodded. Charles smiled. Sandra watched.

Daniel leaned forward and told them, from the beginning all that he had done and experienced. And then he listed the few things that he believed were factual.

"Ah," said Ralph. He looked at Charles.

"Your call," said Charles.

Daniel saw that exchange and wondered about their relationship.

Ralph leaned forward. "Daniel, you have put me in a very difficult situation."

Charles took a swallow from his glass. "Now that is an understatement."

Daniel looked from face to face. "Maybe I should just leave."

Ralph shook his head. "You can't do that, Dan. Not until we decide what to do with you."

Daniel stared at them. "I just came here because I felt, that given who you are, that maybe you have some information that would help me in my research." He shrugged. "If this some kind of security thing, I'll just let it go." He stood.

"Worse than that," said Charles. "Sit down!"

Daniel blanched and did. Worse than? That sounded like some really bad lockup somewhere. His eyes danced around the room, checking whether he would be able to escape or not.

"Don't try," snapped Sandra. She now held a handgun, pointed at him.

"Oh crap," gasped Daniel. Not again. He had been shot that one time. It was not pleasant, not all. "I have just recovered from being shot. O.K.? I will just sit here, very, very still. And you can tell me what to do."

Sandra smiled at him. "Good boy."

Ralph stood. "Would you like something to drink?"

"Red wine would be fine."

Ralph walked from the room and returned with a tray in one hand. It held several glasses. In his other hand he clenched a large wine bottle by the neck. He set the wine bottle on a table.

Handing a glass to Sandra, then one to Daniel, he set the last one and the tray on a small table, and uncorked the wine bottle with an ornate cork puller. Then he filled the three glasses, took the last one and sat.

After taking a sip, then another, Ralph looked at Daniel and nodded.

"We know all about you, Daniel. All about your work in the government and your endeavors with your company. We know how your mind works and what that group you associate with is up to."

Daniel nodded and took a swallow from his glass. It was definitely not low cost stuff. He nodded. Of course they knew. He hadn't expected anything less.

"So, here's the problem, from what you just told us," continued Ralph.

Daniel nodded again. And took another swallow.

"It seems that you have bumped into something that is so secret that only a few of us know it."

Daniel emptied his glass. Worse and worse, he thought. He knew about what Ralph did, in a vague sort of a way. He held out his glass. Might as well. He had no other options.

Ralph stood and refilled it. Then he sat and looked at Charles.

Charles took a big swallow from his glass. And shrugged. "I think that he can be trusted." He smiled at Daniel. "I already saved your life, so to speak."

Daniel gasped. "You put me in my house?"

"Nope," replied Charles. "Not us. All I did was say that you were a nice guy.""

Daniel smiled. "Do you mind if I say that I am confused. What exactly have I done?" This was not what he had hoped they could talk about. Not at all. "And what are you alluding to?"

Ralph leaned back. "You no doubt have heard what happened to William Williams III and his research facility out in the plains?"

Daniel nodded. "Not much. Only that the whole thing was destroyed and all personnel, including Williams, were killed."

"And about some strange happening way out west?

Daniel nodded again. "But again not very well explained."

Charles laughed.

"And," continued Ralph," about our house being attacked and destroyed as well as some people kidnaped."

Daniel slowly nodded and frowned.

"And about my alleged death and the real deaths of my brother and his wife as well?"

Daniel leaned back and stared at Ralph. "Where is all this going?"

Charles stood and walked to the kitchen and came back with a large can, opened, and refilled his glass.

Ralph smiled. "Daniel, it appears that you have bumped into some folk that we are sworn and bound to keep from common knowledge."

Daniel jerked upright. "They are real?"

"Yep," said Charles.

"And they were involved in all those events you just related?"

"Yes," said Ralph. "Mostly."

"O.K." stated Daniel. "I will quit looking." He smiled.

"Not that easy," said Charles.

"Why not?" Daniel stared at him.

"Because," said Ralph. "They are already aware of you."

"WHAT?" Daniel jumped to his feet. It must be The Forest Ghost.

"Sit!" snapped Sandra. She still held the gun pointed at his chest. Her other hand held her glass of wine. She took a sip, eyes watching him carefully.

Slowly he sat. "And what does that mean? Exactly? And who are they? And what do they want with me?"

"Daniel," said Charles. "I have already been visited and asked whether they ought to be worried about you, about your existence."

"My existence?"

"Yep." He frowned at Daniel. "About whether you ought to continue to exist or not."

"Dan," said Sandra. "I know these folk very well, at least as well as one of us could know them. They are very, very private and wish to remain so."

"Like I said, I'll stop! Continue to exist? What are they, some sort of mafia type group?" This was just sounding worse and worse.

Ralph shook his head. "I think that you will have to visit and speak with them, face to face. Sandra?"

She stood, her gun put somewhere. "O.K. Ready to travel, Dan? Stand up."

He stood. She walked close to him. "Relax. And behave."

He frowned at her. What was she talking about?

They were gone.

"Amazing," laughed Charles.

"Dee and her folk spent a long time seeing if they could train Sandra to do that. She is the only one outside of their population that can."

"Hope Daniel has a strong heart. He is in for a shock."

House Darthar.

She stood in front of the outside door, a rather short female, and knocked gently, and waited. It was the polite thing to do.

She looked around at the forest setting. It was a very pleasant place. The door silently opened and he looked out.

She bowed to him.

"Do come in, Tineral." He stepped back and bowed.

She followed him down the interior hallway and into a small, comfortably furnished room.

He poured two cups of coffee and handed her one and

waited until she sat. He sat in the chair next to her and took a sip. And waited. It was the polite thing to do.

She took a sip. And waited.

"Ummmmmm," he said.

"Lord, House Head Aranda sent me to bring another message from House Ritilar."

"Ah, umm."

She told him all that had been sent to her house about the strange behavior of The People in that small People cluster.

He nodded. "The People are always doing strange. The watch thing we rented from Hondo is following and we will know more. But, it is hard to understand that kind of strange behavior. I could speak to Daliera. She has great insight into things like that having been raised as one of them for so long."

"Please do. House Ritilar worries relocation. Strange like that looks dangerous. They are a small house."

"If House Ritilar wishes relocation tell the House Head that House Darthar and House Darthar Na will aid them. But it appears that all that strange has taken itself elsewhere."

Tineral nodded and took a sip from her cup.

House Darthar Na.

They stood in the meadow surrounded by forest. The meadow stretched in a gentle slope to the base of the entry stairs of the many storied structure. The house was half chateau, half fairytale castle. Everything was constructed of light red wood perched on heavy dark green stone foundation walls, roofs of soft brown. The whole thing stretched along the slope rather than up and down the mountain's flank.

They stood near the base of that long staircase.

Daniel gasped.

Sandra grabbed one of his arms. "Don't worry. It is

perfectly normal." She laughed. "In a manner of speaking."

She started up the stair yanking him along by one arm.

Daniel looked down at the large meadow and the forest. "Where are we?"

"No idea. But you are safe as safe can be."

He shook his head. "Explain how we did whatever it was that we did. Please? And why you don't know where we are!"

"Can't. I don't know. Really. I do . . . not . . . know. I do not know how it works either, only that it does." He released his arm and patted him on a shoulder. "It was a gift."

"A gift?"

"Uh huh."

She knocked on the outer door, and waited, patiently.

The door opened in and she peered out. "Do come in, Sandra and, ummmm, friend."

She led them down the main entry hall and told Sandra about the paintings.

"It is really nice," said Sandra.

"A, ummmm ah, strange way for you to come."

Sandra nodded. "I didn't want to shock him too badly."

The trio entered a small room with comfortable chairs and a great outside window that framed the meadow and the surrounding forest. Coffee was poured and handed around. Then all sat.

Sandra took a sip and waited.

"Ummmmmm." Dee took a sip.

"This is Daniel Fanzle."

She stared at him, eyes searching his face and his posture.

He stared back. "You are D. Grant. I saw a picture of you in your publisher's office."

Dee nodded. "I really ought to remove that."

He pointed at Sandra. "She brought me here."

Dee nodded. And looked at Sandra.

"Ralph felt that it was necessary."

"Ah ummmmmmmmm." Dee took a sip and looked at him. "Why?" She frowned.

"He felt that this one would figure it out sooner or later. As House Head of an Adopted House he felt that it would be your decision."

Daniel stared at Sandra. House head? Adopted house? What on earth were they talking about? Decision? About what?

Dee nodded. "We know of you, Daniel Fanzle. Dark Sybil spoke with us."

"Us?" He looked around the room. "Where am I? And how did Sandra do that."

Dee took a sip.

Sandra nudged Daniel and took a sip. He did the same thing.

"This is House Darthar Na,"said Dee. "This is my home. Where in the world is not for you to know. Sandra trained long and hard just to see whether we could give one of The People a house skill. It was a House Darthar skill. The House Head agree to let the skill trainers of each house to work together, just to see if they could teach her that. It worked."

"How do I get back?" He looked around the room and out the window at the large meadow and surrounding forest. None of this made any sense, not at all.

"If we decide that you may leave, Sandra will take you back."

"If? You decide?"

"Most so." Dee took a sip.

"Why wouldn't I be able to leave." He looked from one to the other. Two rather small females. No problem.

"The door will not open for you." Dee nodded. "And you

cannot do anything."

"Really?"

"Most so." She took a sip.

The door to the room flew open and a young woman stepped in holding a tall, thick staff that glowed a soft purple. A very large, white, feline-looking animal followed her into the room and sat, and stared at Daniel.

"Mother, why is one of them here?"

"Tiela, this is the male called Daniel Fanzle. He will behave."

"Ummmmmmmmmmm."

Dee handed her a cup of coffee. "We were just discussing what to do. Sit."

Tiela took a sip and looked at them. "Sandra, most welcome." She leaned the staff in a corner and sat. Now it looked like dark wood.

Daniel stared at it, then at the great white whatever it was and then at Dee. She didn't look old enough to have a daughter as old as Tiela appeared to be.

Dee looked at his ever more puzzled expression. "We talked with Charles and he said that you were a nice person."

Tiela stared at him and appeared to relax.

"Ah, O.K." Whatever that meant, it seemed to mean that he was safe.

"A few of Ralph's, ummmmmm, group know of our existence. This is a unique happening in our long existence. They are sworn to never tell, under any circumstances. It would be a very not nice thing to do."

Sandra gasped. And took a sip from her cup. Ralph hadn't told her something like that.

Daniel stared from Sandra to Dee. "A very not nice thing?"

"Most so," stated Tiela. Her staff suddenly glowed purple.

"Tiela," said Dee. The staff returned to wood.

Daniel stared at it. How could a wooden staff do something like that?

"My daughter felt your presence and came to protect me," explained Dee. She looked at Tiela. "I do not require protection."

Tiela nodded. She set her cup on a table and stood, snatching her staff. "I am going to practice." And left the room followed by her Ice Cat.

"You don't need protection?" Daniel smiled at her.

"Most so."

"I could knock you down and leave, if I wished."

"No. You can not."

He stared at her.

Sandra sighed. "Don't hurt him, Dee. Please?"

Daniel stared at Sandra. Don't hurt him?

Sandra nodded. "Don't."

Daniel stood. "I have to see." He lunged at Dee.

Dee's hand popped out, palm facing him as she thrust. He slammed into the far wall and slid to the floor.

Dee took a sip and watched as he lurched upright. "It is a house skill. A non-lethal house skill."

He stepped carefully over, turned his chair upright, and dropped into it. "I see." Non-lethal? House skill?

"Who, exactly, are you?" he gasped. One shoulder really hurt. He wondered how badly he had hurt it, slamming into the wall that way.

Dee stood. "I am hungry. Come with me and we can get something to eat and talk, you, me, and Sandra."

Washington, D.C.

The phone on Charles' desk buzzed. He picked it up and punched the pulsating red button.

"What?"

He listened. And smiled.

"Bring him right along."

He shoved all the papers on his desk top into a folder, stuffed the folder into the appropriate drawer, locked the drawer, leaned back in his chair, and watched the door to his office.

It was a few minutes walk to his office from the front desk.

And in a few minutes the door was opened by a tall man wearing a large gun in a holster on his hip. "Go right in." He stepped back and waited.

Harold Tridler walked in wearing a grey suit, forty extra pounds, and a worried expression on his face.

"Have a seat, Harold," said Charles, reaching out and pouring two large mugs full of coffee and taking one. "Have some coffee. Relax."

Harold sat in the only chair, which was placed directly in front of Charles' desk. He carefully took the mug and a sip.

"You are here to have a little talk with me," stated Charles. He opened a thin folder and slipped out a number of photographs.

He turned them and spread them out so they could easily be seen. "These are very interesting candid camera shots. Care to tell me what you see going on in them."

Harold leaned forward and stared at them. His face flushed red and then drained of all color. He stared at Charles.

"Better breath deep, Harold. You look like you could be going into shock. Drink your coffee, it might help."

"What?" rasped Harold, "do you want?"

"As a very busy body lobbyist it does appear that you have been paying a couple of folk large amounts of money." Charles shrugged. "Normal for lobbyists, I suppose."

Harold sat and stared at him, mouth slightly open.

"Of course," added Charles. "Doing that with a known criminal like Rasto and doing that with a highly placed politician might mean terrible things to your livelihood as well as to your life style, like where you might be living for a number of years."

Harold gulped his coffee.

Charles shoved the carafe across his desk toward him. "Have some more. I think you need it." He took the cloth covering off the basket on the corner of his desk. "Have a doughnut."

Charles took a chocolate covered one and took a big bite out of it. "They are fresh," he mumbled as he chewed.

Harold leaned back, after taking a cream-filled log, and a small bite from it.

"O.K. Harold, here is what I want to know. Ready?"

Harold nodded. Slowly.

"Who gave you the orders to hire Rasto?"

Harold swallowed loudly. "Him." He pointed at the other photos. "Him."

Charles smiled. "Thought so. Nice to have someone corroborate it." He finished the doughnut and took another. Maple glazed.

"I suspect that the funds going to Tim have something to do with that outfit that is having all those monetary problems after having their government contracts yanked." He took a bite, chewed, and watched.

Harold nodded.

"O.K. Harold, thanks for coming in. Do try and stay out of trouble."

Harold wobbled to his feet. "I am free to go?" He still held the partially eaten cream-filled log.

"Yep." Charles smiled broadly at him. "I just gave you a get-out-of-jail card. Use it wisely." He took another doughnut.

Couldn't let them go stale, could he?

When the door closed behind Harold, Randy walked in from the other room.

"Well, that tells us what we expected," he said.

"Yep. But we still have to wait."

Randy sighed. He was not good at waiting.

Maryland.

They appeared in the living room. The lights were turned low, except for the one by the couch. Soft classical music played from some piece of equipment mounted on the wall.

Ralph set the book he had been reading to one side, bookmark in place, and smiled at his wife. "Good trip."

She dropped next to him and waited. He reached over, handed her a glass, and filled it with red wine, and then topped up his own glass.

Daniel stared at them.

"Wine?" asked Ralph. "Or would you like something else?" He took a small swallow from his glass.

"Scotch?" asked Daniel.

Ralph pointed at a cabinet. "Take whatever you wish."

Daniel opened the cabinet, took a glass and the cap off a bottle and poured the glass full. He walked back and sat in a chair facing the couch. And took a swallow.

"How can you treat this so, ahhhh, normally?"

Ralph smiled. "It is normal. In a manner of speaking."

Sandra poked Ralph with her elbow, gently.

"Uh?"

"Dee said that it is the prerogative of the House Head to accept new members into the house," she stated.

"Oh."

"Yes, Dear."

He looked at Daniel.

"Yes," said Sandra. "He needs to be part of a house."

"I see."

"I knew you would, dear."

"What about you, Daniel? What do you think?"

"I think that my life has truly been changed." He nodded. "But Dee told me why."

Ralph smiled. "Welcome to House Sextet. I chose the name." He looked at Daniel, very hard he looked. "You do understand what that means, I hope."

Daniel nodded. "We had a very long talk over lunch." He smiled. "Guess I won't need to go to any more meetings. All that has been settled. And none of the members will ever know, will they."

"No," said Ralph. "Just like all the rest of the people everywhere."

Daniel took a sip from his glass. "They are very private, aren't they."

"Yes. Once, when we first knew what Dee was, we, just from curiosity, began to search the mythologies, just like you were doing. She felt that we were trying to pry. We came home and found the back door hacked from its hinges, the computers wrecked and dismantled, all our files gone. It was all done before the alarms brought anyone to the place. That is how fast they worked."

"Tell him," said Sandra.

Daniel looked at her and then Ralph.

"Something you need to know and take to heart," said Ralph. "And I am saying this in the most serious way."

'O.K." Daniel took another sip. "Really good stuff."

Ralph smiled. Then his expression became very stern.

"I am sure that Dee didn't say anything like this, but I am

very serious, based upon first hand knowledge. And you absolutely must believe it." He took a swallow from his glass.

Daniel nodded and took a swallow. Now what?

"They are the most dangerous beings that you will ever meet. Anywhere in the world. They are also the most quiet beings that you will ever meet, who hold their privacy in the highest regard. They regard meddling into their affairs as the worst type of behavior. It may be the highest crime there is, in their cultural value system."

"She didn't mention any of that." And wondered why.

Ralph nodded. "They refer to themselves as the Hidden Ones and wish to remain so. They appear to be willing to go to any length to keep that so."

Daniel nodded. "O.K." He looked from face to face. "May I go home now?" He required some time to just think about all that he had been told.

Ralph stood. "Sure. You are free to go and do whatever you want to do. Just remember that you are now bound to their cultural values as well as to your own." He walked over and laid a hand on Daniel's shoulder. "And as the House Head I am now held responsible for your actions." He stepped back. "And I take that very serious, also."

Daniel stood. "I'll remember that." And smiled at Sandra. "Thanks for the trip."

She smiled back. "We'll see you around, Daniel."

It was several days later and The Council had gathered together.

The dining room was paneled in dark wood with wide molding. The thick rug was a deep burgundy. The variable lighting in the room was set at a level pleasing to the eyes. The chairs set around the polished wood table were comfortable with plush cushions and backs. All in all, it was a very relaxing room for lovely meals, delicious desserts, and very nice after dinner libations.

The six of them had just finished dessert and beginning to sip from glasses and mugs whatever their favorite beverage happened to be.

Charles glowered at them. It was a very dark and threatening look.

Ralph stared at him. He knew that expression. Charles was seriously considering some type of mayhem.

"What?" asked Ralph.

"I do not like letting all those crooks walk free!"

"Crooks? Walk free?"

Charles nodded. "You know who I mean. Rasto and Tridler."

Randy took a sip of his very old cognac. And grinned at Charles.

"WHAT?" barked Charles. Randy had a very evil grin on his face.

"Settle down, big guy. They aren't going anywhere."

"What . . . did . . . you . . . do?"

"Wellll," drawled Randy. "For starters, they are not walking anywhere, free or otherwise. I have those two stashed in separate houses with the requisite number of mean and nasty keepers attending to them. Rondak is staying with Rasto just to keep him out of trouble as well."

Charles took a long swallow from his tall glass and then glared at Ralph. "Could have said something," he grumbled.

"Didn't give me time to say anything." Ralph winked at his long-time friend.

"I told them that we weren't going to do anything to them," he grumbled.

Charles took another swallow. "Only that we were going to stop breaking up things for Rasto and that Tridler wouldn't be going to jail. Nothing else."

Sandra refilled Ralph's wine glass. "Randy isn't breaking up things anymore and they both aren't in jail. Yet!"

"Um bum," mumbled Charles.

Randy winked at Sandra. "Charles, they are both being offered the opportunity to testify in court with immunity when we drag that weasel Grimble into court to face a long time in a bad place. We just can't do that yet." He shrugged. "So they are our guests, like it or not, for awhile."

Ralph stood. "Shall we retire to the living room and talk there?"

They followed him there and settled in their usual places with their usual beverages in hand.

Charles told them what little he knew but not how he knew it. They wouldn't ask how.

A Market Town.

Here and there at the edge of the square filled with booths offering all manner of things there were cafes. They all had numbers of tables set around their fronts where folk could sit, eat, drink, hold conversations, and watch the activity in the market.

At one of these tables, set off to one side and rather private, sat a short heavy set man wearing nondescript clothing.

Another man approached, pulled out a chair and sat.

"Hello, Stannis," he said.

"Nilit," said the other, filling two glasses with a deep red wine, locally produced, and pushing one across the small table.

Nilit took a swallow from his glass and smacked his lips. "A good year." He smiled.

Stannis nodded. "Not good news."

"Oh?"

"Some other players are involved, unknown players."

"Why is that a problem?"

"Because they seem to have known what we were looking for. Someone else appears to be handling what you wished to find."

Stannis waggled a hand at the other. "We are tracking them. But I think, from the direction they are heading, that retrieving your package is going to take an organization that has skills well beyond mine."

Nilit took a big swallow of his wine. "My overseas friend is going to be very unhappy."

Stannis shrugged. "All I can do, I will do. All funds can be returned."

Nilit shook his head. "The money is your's. Just tell me whatever you know, when you know it. His upset will not be with you." He stood and pushed a small piece of paper across the table. It contained the names they would use when next they met.

Washington, D.C.

Timothy Grimble charged down the hall. He had to check that things were going as planned. Today he wore a black tie with white stripes on it.

Swinging the door wide, he stepped into his offices. His secretary, as always there before he arrived, smiled at him, stood and handed him a stack of messages, and a number of envelopes still unopened.

He snatched them from her them, quickly poured himself a cup of coffee, and hurried into his space, a large room with windows along one side framing a view of sun-drenched neatly mown grass. And the city beyond. The door slammed behind him, startling his secretary.

Dropping heavily into the chair behind his desk, he sat and swivelled around to face the window, took a swallow from his cup, leaned forward and banged the cup on the window sill, and began to read the messages, dropping them, one by one, into the paper shredder.

Taking another sip from his cup and returning it to its place on the sill, he began to rip open the envelopes with a letter opener. He carefully read each one and then added them to the others in the shredder.

Holding his cup in one hand, he leaned back, both feet on the window sill.

Then he spun back to his desk and banged on the keys, grumbling to himself as the computer slowly brought up the window that he had requested.

He read the message and nodded to himself. Well, not too bad, he thought. Who could be so interested in his business over there? Well, well, well. At least that group had enough sense to move quickly on their own initiative. It was just a matter, now, of agreeing on the price for additional, ah, services rendered.

He swung back to stare out the window. What was taking The President so long to make a decision. It was really quite simple. After all, he had made it crystal clear in his memo. Ah well, there was always the dragging of feet of the political process as it worked at finding a safe way to do things.

Massachusetts.

Swift Nicky Tanagal looked at the large man sitting in the large chair on the other side of his desk.

His eyes watched the other's face.

"You called?" asked Charles.

Swift leaned back, picked up one of the several phones on his desk and spoke to whoever was on the other end, hung up, and waited.

A very wide man walked in, set a file on Swift's desk, and left, gently closing the door behind himself.

Swift opened it and took a quick glance at the paper

"O.K., we were looking at two matters."

Charles nodded.

"On the one matter, Daniel Fanzle, he has returned to the United States, right?"

Charles nodded. It wasn't new information to him.

"On the other matter some people, ah, friends, are slowly following a very twisted trail through a number of places." He frowned. "During that activity it seems that a few more folk seemed to have died." He shrugged. "Guess they were not being helpful to the ones doing the searching."

His eyes stared into Charles. "Sorry, it is taking more time that I thought that it would. But it appears to be getting rather more complicated. These friends are in Europe and they say that what you are concerned about also is, as far as they can tell, still there."

Charles frowned. "Complicated?"

"Indeed. Now there appears to some other group that is getting involved. From all that I have been told, this other group, not those we thought were involved, have moved in and, ahhhhhh, run off with that," he sighed, "package."

Charles almost lurched to his feet. Almost. "Not good, not good at all."

Swift Nicky nodded. And held up a hand.

"But," he said, "my, umm, friends are, eh, tracking this bunch. So, depending upon where they wind up, they might be able to do something about that. At least tell us where."

Charles slumped in his chair. "Worse and worse."

Swift sat just a little straighter. "My, ah, friends thought that this new group that is now involved may think they can make a great deal of money doing this."

"Damnation," snarled Charles. "What we don't need is some gigantic ransom demand popping into the mass media."

Swift shrugged. "Can't help you there, buddy."

Charles sighed. "I know." He stood. "Well, let me know if, or when, you hear anything that might be helpful before this pile hits the fan."

"Of course."

House Darthar.

The four of them sat in comfortable chairs and sipped from their cups of coffee.

Jonathon had served them, it was the polite thing to do as the host.

He took a sip and nodded at Dee. "Tineral is First Daughter of House Fartop. You remember Aranda, House Head."

Dee took a sip and nodded. "He has one of the Tarken."

Tineral smiled. "He is very proud about that."

"Ahhhh ummmmm." Jonathon took a sip.

Hofga grumbled, just a little bit.

"Hofga and I hired a watch thing from Hondo to observe the strange activities of a small People cluster not too far from House Ritilar. The strange behavior of the People cluster was bothering to House Ritilar." Jonathon stood and refilled their cups, then sat.

He took a sip. "Dee, the watch thing will show you what has been going on there. The people are being very strange. We would like to know what they are doing."

She nodded. And took a sip. "Show me."

And then she was there, watching all the interactions

between the People who came in great vehicles and the local People in that small cluster.

Dee stared at Jonathon when it was over. "The young female is being held hostage or captive, something like that. It looks to me as if two, maybe more, groups of the People are trying to be the ones in control of her."

Jonathon took a sip. "Do you recognize the young female."

Dee shook her head. "I really don't pay attention to them, not much any more. Nor do I read any of their many newspapers any more. I have no idea who she is. But I assume that she must be important to someone."

"Ah ummmm." He took a sip.

Dee stared at him.

"It just appears to be more than the usual strange People behavior," he said.

She took a sip and nodded. "Can the watch thing show those events to one of the People?"

"No."

Dee took a sip and then smiled. "I know a way to do that. Perhaps."

Hofga stared at her.

"Ummm," said Jonathon.

Tineral gasped.

Dee stood. "Take me to House Patelan, Jonathon."

He stood and stepped over to her. "Hofga and Tineral will wait here."

They were gone.

Washington, D.C.

Harold Tridler strode the corridors visiting this one or that one of the members of the House of Representatives to advocate for the various interests that he currently represented.

He twitched from a bad case of nerves after his conversation with Charles. Actually, he didn't twitch at all, he just felt that he ought to, his nerves felt so tight. After that conversation he had changed customers, suggesting all the politically acceptable reasons for doing so. It was how the game was played. And now he was talking and arguing about various pieces of legislation that were pending and gathering a hint here and there about another matter of concern.

Now and then he asked, in an ever so careful and oblique manner, about a certain staff person. And slowly, ever so slowly, he was learning things that he felt that certain staff person would be very upset about if he knew that information seemed to be leaking out.

And, like all the good folks in his profession, such as it was, he kept that information to himself. He was slowly, ever so carefully, building a bargaining chip which he could only play once. But he was sure that this one would be greatly to his benefit, when and if he had to play it. Harold was determined that he was going to stay out of jail, regardless of what Charles had told him.

He smiled to himself. He had even started going to gym and working to lose a few excess pounds.

And he was sure, as sure as he had ever been, that there was a rather bad thing going on relative to that certain staff person. And Harold was not going to be anywhere close enough to take any damage when that disaster blew up and damaged everything in reach.

House Patelon.

They stood on a narrow ledge high above the sea. An equally narrow path far to the left worked its way down from the flat headland high above this ledge. The House had relocated to this place in the very long ago.

In front of them the basalt face stretched upward to a rather sharp edge.

Dee knocked on the face next to a small clump of green growth clinging to that face. And waited politely.

A door suddenly appeared and swung inward and a rather wide and short man peered out.

"Daliera Fontala and Jonathon, come to visit," said Dee.

"Ahhhhh, most welcome Daliera Fontala. Do come in, both." He stepped back and led them along a roughly carved tunnel straight back into the rock. The door closed behind them.

Finally, he turned right at a intersection, walked to the second door and opened it, and waved them inside.

Dee and Jonathon entered a wood paneled room with a table and a number of chairs clustered around it. A tall woman rose from her chair and bowed to them.

She smiled warmly. "Most welcome, Daliera, and, ah ummmm."

"Here is Othara, Head of House Darthar. He prefers Jonathon," explained Dee.

The woman bowed to him. "Here is House Head, Nanaloa." She waggled one hand at the chairs. "Do sit." Picking up a tall beaker she poured three cups of coffee and set one in front of each guest before taking the last one and sitting. She took a sip and looked at them.

Dee took a sip, and waited, Then took another sip.

"Ah ummmmm," she said.

Nanaloa took a sip and looked at her.

"I wish to ask a favor," said Dee.

"Favor?"

"Most so."

"What is this favor you would ask?"

"Small and something that is one of your house skills."

"Ummmmm." Nanaloa took a sip.

"I would like a picture drawn of one of the People. Something done quickly."

Nanaloa sucked in her breath and stared at her.

"Of one of the People?"

Dee explained what Jonathon had done with the watch thing hired from Hondo.

"There is a female being held against her wishes. Various small numbers of the People are arguing over her. I would like a very quick portrait of her. I am, ummmm, bothered by all that strange."

Nanaloa sat and sipped from her cup, eyes looking somewhere else. Then she looked at Dee. And nodded.

The door to the room opened and a slender young woman stepped in. "Head?"

Nanaloa explained what Dee would like done. "Will you be able to do this?"

"Most so," she replied.

"Sit then, and ready your materials." Nanaloa looked from Jonathon to Dee. "Here sits Third Daughter, Astal. She is very quick and expresses our house skill close to one of our best ever."

Astal opened the folder she had been holding, pulled a large sheet from it and then set several charcoal sticks taken from her pocket next to it.

She looked at Jonathon. "Have the watch thing show me this young People female."

Jonathon issued instructions and all watched as Astal's hand flew over the sheet, rapidly outlining and then filling in the young woman's features. It didn't take long.

"Amazing," said Dee. She looked at Nanaloa. "She is greatly talented."

Nanaloa bowed her head. And looked up. "Astal, here is Daliera Fontala, Head, House Darthar Na. She asked this favor and owes debt. You may state what you wish."

Astal stared at Dee. "True?"

Dee nodded. "Most so?"

"May I visit?"

"Most so. But, that is true for all of this house. A favor asked is a favor returned. What?"

Astal wobbled her head. And pushed the sheet over to Dee. "I will think deep and visit."

Dee picked up the sheet and bowed to Nanaloa and Astal. "Always welcome. But we must leave now."

Nanaloa stood. "I will walk you to the door."

As they stepped outside, Nanaloa said, "Astal will think deep and ask for little, I do believe. It is her way."

Dee bowed to her. "We will be most pleased for her visit."

The door closed.

Dee turned to Jonathon. "Can you take us to Daniel Fanzle."

Jonathon nodded. "I have the name and he has the Feyra touch."

A sea gull coasted through the space where they had been standing.

Maryland.

As was the custom of the group, they had a great dinner and dessert. Now they were scattered around in the living room, each in their favorite place, sipping their favorite beverage. It was time to discuss some aspects of business.

They were meeting in the home of Charles and Prentice.

All the rooms were much less formal in decor than the home of Ralph and Sandra.

Richlin, the daughter of Charles and Prentice, was at some movie with some friends.

Charles looked at Ralph.

"Well," said Ralph. "This are getting a little tense. Seems he, they all knew who "he" was, has heard that there is a group searching, also searching, in and around the area that some folk had heard about. This group appears to not be worried about folk dying as they make their search. But, so far, not much but some vague stories."

Charles refilled his tall glass from a large can and looked at Ralph after he took a swallow. "Those folks, the ones with the, ah, casual approach, are known to Swift Nicky who has asked them, as a favor, to see if they can track down that young woman. They, ummmm, tracked her to some tiny burg in a very isolated valley. But some new crowd had been there, shot up the place, and took her elsewhere. Swift's acquaintances are following and will report to him what they find."

Randy jerked and stared at Charles. "Those guys reliable?"

Charles laughed. "You betcha."

"Oh," said Ralph.

All eyes swivelled toward him.

"He also told me that one of our Consular people had been approached about buying a very important package."

"Hell in a hand basket," snapped Randy. "I trust whoever that was has enough sense to keep this as quiet as quiet can be!"

Ralph nodded. "He was flown to D.C. where he is being kept under wraps."

Randy sighed. And took a sip from his glass.

The doorbell rang.

Charles jumped up. "I'll get it." He hurried down the short hall and threw open the front door.

"Hello, Charles," said Daniel Fanzle.

Charles glared at the trio standing there, ever so patiently.

"If this isn't going to complicate things, I don't know what will. Do come in, all." Charles stepped back.

He stepped back and led them to the living room where they had stares and frowns directed at them.

Dee sat on the couch next to Sandra, who stood. "I'll get the coffee pot and some cups." She hurried to the kitchen.

Daniel walked over, opened a cabinet and poured some brandy into a tall glass, turned and smiled at Ralph, and took an appreciative sip.

Ralph nodded. And waited. Sandra returned, filled the two cups, handing one to Dee and one to Jonathon, and then sat next to Dee again.

"What?" asked Ralph.

Daniel handed him a large sheet of paper. "Recognize this young woman?"

Ralph took it, nodded, and passed it to Charles.

"Who drew this?" Ralph refilled his wine glass.

Charles grumbled something.

Daniel looked at Dee.

"Astal, Third Daughter of House Patelon," said Dee.

Randy stared at her. And wondered what kind of hippy outfit that was.

Ralph held up his hand, stopping all questions forming.

"She saw this young woman?" asked Ralph.

"No," stated Dee. "But the young woman was in a small People cluster in a very isolated area. Daniel marked several places on his map where he thought it might be located."

Daniel unfolded a large map and spread it out on a handy table. The map had several red circles scrawled on it.

"Was?" asked Randy. He wondered how anyone could draw such a accurate portrait and not see them. Ralph was staring at the floor between the tips of his shoes, frowning deeply.

"Most so," stated Dee. "A large group of very not nice People took her from that place."

Daniel pointed. "Not many roads going anywhere in these spots.

Jonathon sipped his coffee and watched all the others. Then he looked at Dee.

"Ah ummmmm." She took a sip.

"What?" Ralph looked from her to Jonathon and back again.

Dee took a sip. "When those not nice ones finally stop and put her somewhere, I, we, will be able to tell what that place looks like. Perhaps Daniel will know this place." She nodded at him. "In the very recent past he has been wandering all through that region."

Randy lurched to his feet, started to say something, and crashed back into his chair.

Dee looked at him. "No, I will not tell you how." She stood, as did Jonathon.

Daniel smiled at her. "I think that I will stay awhile and talk with Ralph. Thanks."

She nodded and the pair headed down the hall and out the front door.

Shortly thereafter the group broke up and went to their various homes or offices.

Shafts of morning sunlight pouring through the kitchen windows made bright squares on the floor and tickled her bare feet.

Ralph, his adopted daughter Sandrel, and Daniel, their overnight guest, sat and watched Ralph's wife, Sandra, making breakfast. It was her feet that should have gotten tickled. She didn't notice. She was wearing slippers.

None of the watchers offered to help. It had been explained to Daniel that Sandra preferred to do the cooking by herself.

She gave the scrambled eggs a last stir and set the large skillet on the table on the wooden and ornately carved place for it.

Ralph passed around the toast while Sandra served everyone. Then Ralph filled their coffee cups.

As the last bit of eggs and the last piece of toast were being eaten, Ralph looked at Daniel. "Don't try to understand them, Daniel. They are a totally different species and culture. Many of the aspects of their abilities they don't truly understand. Dee told me that Jonathon had tried to find out and finally gave up, deciding that it was all explained by mutations unique to them."

He refilled his cup. "Jonathan believes that mutation, which he feels mutated several times during their early development, gave them their unique abilities. But it also gave them an extremely long life span and a very widely spaced birthing of their children. That fact is why they are such a small population and why they have such a high regard for their offspring."

Ralph laughed. "Early on they had a great turmoil among themselves with the result being that they would not be doing things as the people were doing. They watched us, Homo sapiens, spreading like wildfire across the globe, fighting and warring and causing great destruction. Thus, they do not to interact with us at all, with some exceptions. Dee was raised by her parents as one of the people, so she has a background of understanding on our behavior. She is unique in that aspect. Almost."

Sandrel stood. "Time to take a walk." She headed for the front door followed by Shadowfog, her black German Shepherd. She bent, hooked on the leash and called, "Bye, Daniel." And headed out for their walk.

Daniel held out his cup. Ralph refilled it.

"I am really and truly confused," stated Daniel.

Ralph laughed. "Not to worry. About them, I am that way most of the time." He stood. "Time to go to work." He winked at Daniel. "Stay and talk with Sandra, if you wish. She might be able to help cut through some of your confusion."

Washington, D.C.

He strolled down the hallway, dressed in his usual dark blue suit, very expensive, neatly tailored, matching light blue shirt, red tie this time, passing offices that were mostly quiet in this early part of the evening. Now and then he waved and smiled at the few hard workers that were finishing up in order to be ready for the next morning's burst of activity and meetings that were the normal part of doing business here in the center of the nation's government.

As he turned through the main intersection toward his offices a man passed him.

The man smiled at him in passing. "Evening, Tim." And headed for the President's office. He was carrying one of the those large things in which artists hauled their drawings around.

Timothy Grimble hesitated for a few steps and then started walking again, brows furrowing in thought, if not worry.

What was he doing here? This late? He chewed his lip. Only that one person could stroll so nonchalantly down this hall, stroll so casually in and out of the President's Office, at any time of the day or night.

Then he shrugged and opened the door to his office suite,

his private domain. Everything was proceeding according to his plan, little by little, inch by inch, with nothing leaking to the beasts of the media. So far so good, in spite of the confusion going on over there. But he felt confident that his contacts would soon clear up that matter. It was, as usual, all a matter of money. And he had the funds to take care of that. And they knew it.

Timothy turned in the doorway and waited. What was Ralph Fredrickson up to now? Then he stared up the corridor and checked his watch. Five minutes, he was only in there for five minutes. Ralph strolled casually down the hall, smiled. "Evening again, Tim." And headed for the outside door. He wasn't carrying that large folder.

Maryland.

Shafts of afternoon sunlight decorated that end of the kitchen and made bright squares on the floor.

Ralph and his adopted daughter, Sandrel, sat and watched his wife Sandra finishing the chili.

Neither of the watchers offered to help as both knew that Sandra preferred to do the cooking by herself.

As she sampled the mixture, made a slight addition to the seasoning, and gave the contents of the large cast iron kettle a last stir, the front door banged open and slammed shut.

"Oh boy, brunch," laughed Charles as he walked into the kitchen. "Or perhaps, lunch."

Ralph pulled over another chair.

Sandrel stood and fetched another large bowl and added more crackers to the basket and smiled at him as he dropped into the appropriate chair.

The four of them put a rather large dent into the contents of the kettle and eliminated most of the crackers.

"So, how you doing, kiddo?" asked Charles as he set his

spoon inside his bowl. He had added a rather large quantity of hot sauce to his portions, smiling happily.

"Fine," replied Sandrel, standing. Charles asked her the same question every time. "Time to take a walk." She headed for the front door followed by Shadowfog, her black German Shepherd. She bent, hooked on the leash and called, "Bye, Charles." And headed out for their walk.

"Ummmm," said Charles, holding out his cup so Sandra could refill it.

"That drawing caused a certain amount of relaxation. It was her, looking quite healthy, given everything," stated Ralph.

"Do we know anything else?" asked Charles.

"Not much," replied Ralph. "Yet! We still don't know where she is, now."

Charles nodded. "Swift has people looking very hard. But with this new group getting involved they are having to, more or less, start over, sorta."

Ralph looked at Sandra. "Think that she would tell you anything. Dee certainly didn't confide anything to Daniel."

Sandra shrugged. "Hard to say. You know how guarded they are."

"Yep," said Ralph.

Sandra stood. "I'll go and ask. See ya, Charles." She walked into the hall, and was gone.

"I am always amazed," said Charles.

Ralph refilled their cups. "Me too."

House Darthar Na.

Dee was sitting with her two daughters, Tiela and Winala, eating a late meal and talking about this and that, mainly how their studies were coming along. As was the usual case, given the topic under discussion, Tiela was frowning darkly and Winala was explaining in happy detail. The two Ice Cats sat to just one side and slightly behind their adopted daughter. And watched the food very carefully.

The door to the room opened and she walked in.

"Sandra," said Dee. "Join us." She poured and handed her a filled coffee cup.

Sandra sat, took a sip. "Just had lunch. Thanks." She waited for their discussion to finish.

After the daughters and the Ice Cats had left, Dee looked at her. "Ummmmm."

"How did you know what that young woman looked like?"

"Jonathon heard about a small House that was being bothered by some strange People behavior inside the small People cluster that the House traded with. After discussing this with Hofga, they rented a watch thing from Hondo just to see what was happening."

"Watch thing?"

Dee smiled. "There are only a very few houses that have that skill, creating things, things with various, ummm capabilities. Hondo is one of the very few." She held up her hand. "A watch thing does just that. It watches and reports, visually, to the one who rented it, what it was rented to watch. None of the people would ever be able to see one of the things. They have the consistency of almost not there smoke and the ability to merge with shadows and other aspects of the environment."

"A house was bothered and Jonathon and Hofga wanted to know why?"

Dee took a sip. "Most so."

"Why did you have a portrait drawn?"

"Jonathon saw the great turmoil between the People of that small cluster and those other very not nice People who took her away from the others. He asked me to watch and give him my opinion about what was going on."

Sandra held out her cup. Dee refilled it.

Dee took a sip. "I knew that Daniel had been wandering about in the general area and thought maybe he might know who she was. It appeared as if she was being held against her wishes." She shrugged. "The People are always doing violent things to each other. As you know I was raised as one of the People. It felt to me to be not nice. So I had the portrait made and showed it to Daniel. Who became greatly agitated and wanted to show it to Ralph."

She took a sip and looked at Sandra. "Why do you care?"

"This is," she took a sip, "a very not nice thing and it is causing a great bother to us. A bother than we are still trying to resolve. We already know a number of the folk involved but not all of them."

"A great bother caused by some very not nice People?" Dee took a sip and frowned. "It there danger to Sandrel? Or others of House Sextet?"

Sandra jerked. "NO!" She took a sip. "No," she said in a calmer tone of voice. "No, not too us, not at all. It is larger problem." She didn't think that it would be a good idea to have Dee deciding to take action of some sort.

Dee nodded. "If Ralph asks for help, perhaps we may be able to do something." She took a sip. "All is well then, inside the house?"

Sandra laughed. "Oh, yes. Sandrel enjoys going to school and has friends from there. Charles' daughter, Richlin, has been telling her about college. We will see that Sandrel will be able attend where ever she wishes to go."

Dee nodded. As Sandra stood, Dee said, "Tell Ralph what we talked about."

Sandra nodded, set her cup on the table, and was gone.

Rugged and Isolated.

Batu had handled the financial matters of the group with an iron control and over their evening meal was discussing it with them and what he felt that they ought to do. He felt that after they get paid for the last job they ought to return home, in ones and twos, and spend a year relaxing and planning what they ought to do next.

While members of the group had returned to visit their home villages in the past, the process was carefully managed and designed to never call attention to that area. One by one, widely spaced in time, they returned to visit, to leave a small amount of financial support. This support was deliberately calculated to make life just that little bit of improvement that was possible for folk living in such isolation but never beyond that. The three villages understood and accepted that. They understood and accepted because they were proud of the activities of their sons and the care they took to keep harm far away.

Now, he suggested, it was time for them all to go home. And plan their future.

In this region of rugged terrain they had found and bought it. It was an up thrusting conical hill, more than hill, less than mountain, standing by itself. A narrow path crawled in a spiral up the steep slope to the summit to where the real prize sat.

An ancient stone structure encased the top. It had obviously been placed to watch over the surrounding land. Batu had inspected it and found that, much to his surprise, that they could easily repair the roofs and in a relatively short time bring the place up to minimal standards, sufficient to suit their needs.

They had done this, in between jobs. The few outside windows had inside shutters which blocked any light from escaping in the evening. While they still used candles in some rooms, the dining area had electric lights. A small, very quiet generator supplied the electricity.

One of their members returned and sat at his place and began to serve himself.

"She is well?" asked Batu.

He nodded, mouth full.

"Untouched?"

He jumped to his feet, crossed his arms over his chest, and swallowed. "Absolutely! On my sacred honor." He bowed, and sat down. "She thanked me for bringing her the food and said that it was much better than where she had been."

Batu smiled. It was good. That young woman was worth a very great deal of money to them. Untouched. Not harmed in any manner. It was good that she was eating.

Maryland.

He stood on the front steps and knocked on the door and waited.

The house looked, more or less, like all the other houses in this area of moderately-sized, moderately priced houses.

The grass was neatly trimmed, the house was always well maintained. All in all, it was just one house among all the others with neatly trimmed lawns and well maintained exteriors.

The door swung in and he looked out.

"Well," boomed Charles, "this is a surprise. Come in, come in."

Charles led him into the living room and turned off the program, a sports event.

Prentice looked up from the book she had been reading. She had learned how not hear whatever Charles was watching. Their daughter, Richlin, was upstairs working on some project of her's.

"Prentice." Charles smiled broadly at her. "This is my long time friend reaching back to my grade school years. This is Swift Nicky Tanagal." He pointed at a table. "Red wine, if you wish some."

Swift stepped over, filled a glass, and smiled. "Pleased to meet you. Mrs. James."

Charles dropped into a chair and picked up his tall glass.

"I never expected to see you here."

Swift sat close. "Me neither, Charles." He looked around the room, checking this and that.

"Nothing here to worry about here," said Charles. "This house is more secure than most places, if not more secure than them all."

Swift leaned back and took a small swallow of the red wine. "Nice."

Then he sat up. "I heard from my friends in Europe."

Charles sat straight. "What's happening?"

"My friends told me that the ones had have that package are a rather ambitious group of bandits, robbers, mercenaries with a heavy streak of mayhem. They came from further east and have apparently taken on some sort of mythical overtones which makes them hard to reason with."

He took another small swallow of the red wine. "My friends say that no-one will oppose them or attempt to take a, ummm, contract that they are interested in. I felt that you should know this right away."

He set the glass on a table and stood. "Pleased to meet you, Mrs. James." He smiled at Charles. "I have to go. You know how that is." And waggled one hand at them. "I will let myself out. See ya, buddy."

He turned, walked down the short hall and out their front

door.

"Charles?"

He took a swallow from his tall glass. "Swift, Ralph, and I were friends from the lower grades through college and there after. His first name is really Swift. He explained that it was a family tradition that stretched back a number of generations."

"Why has he never visited before?"

Charles laughed. "The three of us are in different businesses. I usually meet him on his territory."

Prentice stared at him.

Charles shrugged. "Just different sides of the fence. He often helps us find out things that we might not be able to. But when he does there is no quid pro quo, ever. He would be insulted if we even suggested he might be trying something like that. Just friendship, that's all."

He stood. "I better phone Ralph and let him know. This is going to make things difficult, to say the least."

Washington, D.C.

He strolled down the hallway, dressed in his usual dark blue suit, very expensive, neatly tailored, matching dark blue shirt, dark blue tie with tiny white stars this time, passing offices that were mostly quiet in this early part of the evening. Now and then he waved and smiled at the few hard workers that were finishing up in order to be ready for the next morning's burst of activity and meetings that were the normal part of doing business here in the center of the nation's government.

He shrugged as he pondered the next thing to do and opened the door to his office suite, his private domain. Everything was proceeding according to his plan, little by little, inch by inch, with nothing leaking to the beasts of the media. So far so good, in spite of the confusion going on over there. But he felt confident that his local contacts would be able to take care of this new operation. They knew that they would earn a good reward, untraceable money. He had the funds to take care of that.

Sitting at his desk, he opened the special window on his computer and sent instructions as well as the better than normal amount to their account. He leaned back and nodded. And that should take of that!

Maryland.

Ralph had relocated from his home office to the dining room table, a much larger space to spread out all the materials that he was pouring through.

It was mid-afternoon and he had reached the end of the pile, once again. Finished, he grabbed the carafe and refilled his coffee cup, leaned back, sighed, and took a swallow.

For some reason things were murky. Usually, this far long, he would be seeing a solution of some sort. He took another swallow. Maybe they were being too circumspect. He stared at one of the paintings on the wall. Not much help there. It was just a very pretty meadow replete with birds and butterflies and sunlight. So he leaned way back and focused on the ceiling and thought over everything that they knew and began to shove the pieces around and around in his mind. It was just one more jigsaw puzzle to solve.

The front door banged open, the door slamming against the wall and then shut, and Charles charged into the room. "I AM GOING TO DO BAD THINGS TO BAD PEOPLE!"

Ralph straightened up and stared at him. "What?"

Charles shot past into the living room, opened a cabinet, and filled a glass from the first bottle he grabbed, and came back, sipping as he came. He dropped into the chair next to Ralph.

"Someone is going too far," he growled.

"Oh." Ralph's eyes studied his friend's face very carefully. From that expression he knew that whatever it was, it was going to be very bad.

Charles took a swallow and shoved the glass away.

"I have on my hands two shot up people and one dead stranger whose identity we will know soon. Ralph . . . "

"What, Charles?"

Charles took a deep breath and settled down, a little.

"They snatched your daughter from the playing field at her school. She was practicing her soccer skills with her team. I had one man watching from the bleachers, one wandering around the edge of the field, and a woman sitting with the coaches and watching. Five guys came hurtling from the park adjacent to the field knocking kids every which way. The lead guy grabbed her and started off surrounded by the others. My guys started for them and three of those thugs dropped to one knee and starting firing. Kids and coaches ran every which way, mostly getting into the way. One shooter went down but my guys got hit. The female agent ran into the field and shot two more of the gang but they managed to make it to a dark blue van. She radioed it in and we blocked off the area in a series of concentric circles. So, whoever those guys were, we will have our hands on them soon. I hope. Lots of space to cover."

Ralph gently touched Charles arm. "Your troops going to be all right?"

"Sure. Not too bad. Waiting for the final doctor's report. But I have some very unhappy folk on my hands."

Charles looked at his friend. "I, ahhh, phoned Swift on the way over. His crew might be able to find out faster than we can."

Ralph stood. "I'll talk to Sandra." He headed for his office to make the call. "Let's wait in the living room."

Charles headed that way. Ralph was always calm, at least

on the outside.

In the living room Charles selected one of the large chairs with a high curved back. It would be a good place to be when Sandra came home. He decided that it was as secure and safe a chair as he could find.

House Darthar Na.

Dee was sitting with her two daughters, Tiela and Winala, eating a late lunch and talking about this and that, mainly how their studies were coming along. As was the usual case, given the topic under discussion, Tiela was frowning darkly and Winala was explaining in happy detail.

The door to the room opened and she walked in.

"Sandra," said Dee. "Join us." She poured and handed her a filled coffee cup.

Sandra sat, took a sip. And waited.

Dee finished her discussion with Winala and looked across the table.

"Ummmmm." She took a sip.

Sandra set her cup down. "Bad news, Dee, very bad news."

"About?" asked Dee. Tiela and Winala stared at Sandra.

So Sandra explained all that she had been told by Charles and then took a sip. And waited.

"Tiela," snapped Dee. "Go tell Armilin and Kitea to come here. Winala, upstairs to the beast quarters and send Purr Cat down here. Hurry, please." She took a sip and looked at Sandra. "These are very not nice People, taking Sandrel."

Sandra nodded. "I think we can agree on that."

"You will help me free your daughter."

Sandra nodded again. It hadn't been a statement or question. It had been a command. She took a sip and waited.

Dee watched the door and took a sip.

Armilin, Kitea, and Tiela burst into the room.

Armilin and Kitea bowed to Dee, ignoring Sandra completely.

"Word?" said Armilin, using the formal title of the one that directed The Fontala.

"I want The Fontala ready for anything. Some very not nice People have taken the First Daughter of House Sextet, Sandrel."

"As the Word is said, so shall it be." Armilin spun and ran from the road and up the stairs to the floor where The Fontala lived.

"Kitea, I want The Seventh Stand ready to travel as fast as possible. Gather in the meadow, I will meet them there."

Kitea spun and hurtled from the room just as a large lion-sized, cougar-looking, feline with bronze fur and white tiger stripes of her neck and shoulders slipped on silent paws into the room.

Dee stood and headed for the outside door trailed by Purr Cat and Sandra.

At the bottom of the entry stairs Dee sat on the bottom step and waited. And looked at Sandra.

"Why did those not nice ones do that?" she asked Sandra.

"We don't really know that, Dee. Ralph suspects that it has to do with another matter that The Council has been working on for some weeks now." She shrugged. "Until we can talk with someone from that group to ask, we won't know. Probably. Charles asked a friend of his and Ralph's who might be able to find out where those guys are holed up."

So they sat and waited. But not for long.

Armilin ran down the stairs and bowed to Dee. "The Fontala ready themselves."

Then Kitea charged down the staircase accompanied by Anagon, The One Who Remembers for the Seventh Stand, and Yallan, The Seeker.

They stopped and bowed to Dee.

"The Seventh Stand is here," announced Kitea, the First Hand, the head of the Seventh Stand, as the stream of men and women ran down the stairs, each wearing a dark purple jacket and holding a long staff that glowed with a deep purple light. Tiela was among them as she was a member of The Seventh Stand.

Dee stood and watched as all the other stands assembled and waited. They were dressed as the others, each one holding their long staff, called The Flaming Swords by some of The Fontala.

Armilin stepped over to Dee and bowed. "As was said, so are we here."

"Sandra," said Dee, "take myself, Purr Cat, and Yallan," she indicated the slender male, "to your house. The Fontala will wait here."

Sandra nodded.

Maryland.

"Whoa!" laughed Charles, setting his tall glass on the table next to his chair as he stood.

Dee smiled at him and bowed to Ralph. "We are here to bring back your daughter."

Sandra walked into the kitchen to make a pot of coffee.

Purr Cat slipped over to Charles and gave him a bump with her head.

"Heya," said Charles. He had met her before.

Yallan bowed to Sandra and then Ralph.

"Yallan is a seeker," said Dee. "It is a very rare skill that allows him to know when one of us is near."

Ralph smiled at Yallan. "How close do you have to be?"

Yallan looked at Dee.

"Approximately one of your miles as the People measure distance," said Dee. "So, if you can get us close to where you think Sandrel might be, he will be able to tell."

Ralph waved his hand at the furniture. "Might as well sit and relax. We haven't gotten information that will bring us that close to the kidnappers."

"Yet!" Charles sat and picked up his tall glass and took a swallow.

Dee sat and nodded and took a filled cup from the tray Sandra had just carried into the living room from the kitchen. And sipped. Then she sent a call to Jonathon.

Yallan took a cup and sat in a chair next to Dee and took a sip and then nodded to Sandra. She set the tray on a table and took the third cup. And sat next to Ralph and took a sip.

Charles jerked and stared at a corner of the room where a thick shadow apparently had just formed.

Jonathon stepped out. "Dee?"

Sandra hurried back into the kitchen to bring another cup and the pot of coffee out.

Jonathon pulled a chair close to Dee and then took the cup Sandra handed him. He took a sip.

"Ummmmmm." Jonathon looked at Dee.

"I may require one or more of the Stands of The Fontala."

"Ahhhh ummm." He took a sip.

"We are waiting to see," Dee explained.

Massachusetts.

Swift Nicky Tanagal hung up the phone and looked at the large man sitting in the large chair on the other side of his desk.

His eyes watched the other's face.

"O.K., Alec," said Swift, "this is how the game is going to be played!"

Alec, Swift's number one and long time associate nodded, and frowned, just a little. The expression on Swift's face told him that someone, or someones, were going to have a very painful existence in the near future.

"I want everyone, absolutely everyone, to carry the message everywhere that we have personnel to do so."

Alec nodded again. It was worse that he had suspected.

"People should know the following. I want the names and location of the idiots that took Ralph's daughter. The ones that can tell me this I will owe a big favor, a really big favor."

Alec's eyebrows shot up. Even worse.

"In addition, I want them all to know that I see this kidnaping as a personal insult, as a very grave personal insult, as a very grave personal and family insult!"

Alec stood. "Right away, if not faster!" He spun and ran from the room shouting for his assistants to gather around. Then he explained, very clearly, what he wanted done and what Swift had said to tell those folks that they would be contacting. "I want results now! Not tomorrow or the next day. NOW!"

He watched them hurtle from the room. Then he dropped into his chair and picked up one of the several telephones on his desk. And began to make a number of calls. Finally, he leaned back and thought that this was really going to stir up a whole lot of folks and organizations. Some would just go to ground and hope that they were not visited by very nervous people carrying big guns. Others would do all they could to help. Swift should be hearing something very soon.

Alec picked one of the other phones and placed his order. Soon, in thirty minutes or less, they would deliver boxes of sandwiches and containers of coffee. Every one who delivered any message would eat two sandwiches and take a container of coffee with them to drink on their way to wherever they were headed next.

They knew that they had better hurry.

Maryland.

It was 6:00 a.m.

Ralph, always an early riser, was up, had made a pot of coffee, and now sat at the kitchen table drinking coffee and reading reports.

Halfway through the thick stack he felt his cell phone vibrate.

Taking a small swallow of his coffee, he turned it on. "Yes?"

"Yes, always up first, as you know. What's up?"

"Hold it, getting a clean sheet of paper." He dragged one over, tucked the phone into his shoulder and held the paper with his left hand and his pen with the right.

Then he began write everything that he was told.

Finished, he set the pen down and grabbed the phone in his free hand. "We owe you, buddy." And laughed. "We really ought to have you and your's over for dinner. It will be safe." And laughed again. "Yah, I know. Thanks again."

He hung up and leaned back, refilled his cup, took a swallow, and reread his notes.

And wondered how they had found out, so fast. We really ought to have them working for us. Of course, that was not possible, but it was a thought.

Dee walked in. She had been sleeping in one of the guest rooms. Purr Cat trailed along behind her.

Ralph filled a cup and handed it to her.

"Early riser," he said.

She sat, nodded, and took a sip. "Jonathon will come if we need him. He went home after we talked a bit."

Ralph took a sip and waited.

"Ummmm." Dee took a sip.

"What?"

"You look like you know something." She smiled at him.

He nodded. And took a sip. "Yes, I do. I know where Sandrel is being held." He refilled his cup.

"As soon as Charles arrives and we can all eat breakfast, you, him, me and, umm, Yallan will take a little drive and take a look at the place." He stood and began to take things from the refrigerator.

"Purr Cat will also come along."

Ralph picked up his phone and pushed a button, then another.

He took another sip. "Morning, big guy. We know where. Get over here and have something to eat. Oh, and bring your big truck." He laughed. And looked at Dee. "He is on his way."

Sandra strolled in, wrapped in a soft yellow robe.

"Heard you," she said to Ralph, and looked at all the things he had placed on the counter next to the stove. "I'll start making lots of breakfast."

The Garden Tower.

They stood just inside the tree line and looked across the grass at the structure.

It was a twelve story, square, apartment complex, with a roof garden, set in the middle of acres of well maintained grass. The open space was edged by the wide and dense belt of trees.

Dee stepped out and said, "Ralph, you and Charles wait here. Yallan, Purr Cat, and I will take a little wander around that building and see whether your information is correct." She laughed. "Not one will see Purr Cat. As I told you long ago, you might call her species, the Furleen, Chameleon Cats."

Dee started across the grass toward the tower, Yallan walking by her side. Purr Cat seem to fade into the grass.

As they wandered around the building Yallan stopped. "There is a Feyra in that building." He indicated a window on the top floor. "Right up there."

Sandrel laughed. She had been standing in front of the window in the bedroom they had placed her in. The man young, who had just stepped into the room carrying a tray of food, stopped. "Something funny out there?"

She turned around and smiled at him. "No. Just a bit of happiness." She pointed at the table. "Just put that there."

He did.

She nodded. "You have been very kind."

"Thanks," he mumbled.

"A piece of advice."

"Huh?"

"If I was you I would leave this place and go somewhere else. Now!"

"O.K., Miss, thank you." He turned walked out and shut the door. It was never locked. There was no way she could escape. She didn't have a key card for the elevator or the fire escape doors. He shrugged. And wondered why she had said that to him.

Sandral sat at the table and ate her meal and looked out the window. And watched them walking toward the door that opened onto the restaurant. She had recognized the slim figure dressed in black.

Dee walked into the restaurant and headed over to the stairs down to the tunnel entrance and where the bank of elevators were. She had looked at the plans of the building that Charles had brought with them.

She pointed at the one labeled 12. "Go up there and guard her. We will come late in the evening."

Purr cat slipped over the wall next to that elevator door and faded into the wallpaper.

Dee and Yallan headed down the tunnel toward the parking structure.

Maryland.

They sat around in the living room and talked.

Charles looked at Dee. "Where's your cat?"

Dee took a sip from her coffee cup. "She will be with Sandrel and guard her from those not nice People."

"How?"

Dee smiled. "She will wait until someone opens that elevator door and then she will go up."

Charles stared at her. "She will?"

"Yes." Dee took another sip. "I sent a call to Jonathon to bring the Seventh Stand of The Fontala. They will be needed."

Ralph refilled his glass and Sandra's with a deep red wine.

He took a small swallow. "How many is that?"

"Three hands and three, or in the People's way of counting, eighteen."

"Going to be a full house." Charles laughed. He picked up his cell phone and tapped a few buttons. "I need you to send enough vans to transport, twenty, ah, maybe a few more than that. Right now." He hung up.

Dee took a sip. "We will wait until the middle of the night."

The Garden Tower.

Sandrel had watched Dee and the other one headed into the restaurant and wondered when they would come and get her from this place.

After she didn't see any other thing happening out there, she sat on the edge of her bed and began to read a book. Her captors had brought several, one of which she thought might be a good read.

Time passed.

She heard the elevator ping and its doors slide open. She knew that the elevator would stay like that until someone entered and pushed a down button and swiped their card or someone down below used their swipe card to call it.

She went back to her book. And sat up. There was a suddenly large amount of shouting and hollering going on. Sandrel closed her book, set it on a table, and waited. Maybe all that racket meant that Dee was rescuing her.

The door to her room flew open and one of the men ran in. "Any one other than you in here?"

"No."

He charged over and ran into her bathroom, then ran out and opened the closets in the room, sticking his head into each. "O.K., nobody here." He hurtled out the open door of the bedroom and slammed it shut.

Purr Cat appeared, sitting in front of Sandrel. Sandrel lurched forward and threw her arms around the feline's neck.

"How did you get in here?" She laughed. "But I am really glad to see you?"

When she let go and stopped stroking the thick fur, Purr Cat stood, walked over to a spot in the corner, sat, looked at Sandrel, and faded into the wallpaper, or so it seemed.

The door to her room flew open again.

"Who's in here with you?"

"No one."

"Then who were you talking to?"

"Myself." Sandrel laughed softly. "What was all that noise about?"

"None of your business!"

He backed out and slammed the door shut.

She picked up her book and began to read again. Somehow she felt that Purr Cat was responsible for whatever all that commotion was.

Massachusetts.

Swift Nicky Tanagal looked at the large man sitting in the large chair on the other side of his desk.

His eyes watched the other's face.

"What, Alec?" said Swift

Alec, Swift's number one and long time associate nodded, just a little. They had just wound up a discussion of today's business and were about to leave.

"Something you ought to hear."

"O.K."

Alec stood, walked across the room, opened the door, and leaned out. "Come on in."

He walked back and sat down, swiveling his chair to watch.

The man that walked in was one of those people that were totally normal looking in all ways. It was his primary skill. That, and getting people to talk to him.

"Tell him," said Alec.

"Do," added Swift. "You can sit if you wish."

The man shook his head. "I heard, here and there, a thing about that group you were interested in finding. Ahhh, the one that you found."

Swift nodded.

"It seems," began the man, "that two of their boys were killed this afternoon."

"And?" prompted Swift.

"They were killed inside their private elevator. They were found when the elevator got to their floor and the doors opened. Now that group is very, very excited, and trying to find out how that could happen. That elevator is a very secure thing. At the moment, they are sending a few of their troop out to try and find out which other gang is responsible and trying to muscle in on them. Ahhhh, with no success, so far."

"Why tell me this?" Swift stared at him.

"Just thought that you should know, that's all."

"O.K.," said Swift. "Thank you."

The man hurried from the door and shut the door.

"What do you think?"

Alec shook his head. "No idea. Pretty strange though."

Swift stood. "Certainly is." He headed for the door. "See you tomorrow."

The Garden Tower.

The voice whispered softly.

"Sandrel . . . "

"Sandrel . . . "

"Sandrel . . . "

Her eyes popped open. She looked at the clock on the small table next to the bed, at its glowing red numerals.

2:00 a.m.

She sat up and stared at the figure standing next to the bed.

"Who are you?"

"Here is Yallan, the Seeker, of The Seventh Stand of The Fontala. We have come to take you from these very not nice People."

She rolled from bed. She had been sleeping in her clothes since she had been taken.

"How are you going to do that?" Then she felt the gentle breeze blowing into her room. She stared at the window. It didn't open.

"I removed the window," said Yallan.

She walked over. True. The window was gone. So was some of the wall all around where the window had been.

She turned and looked at him. "How did you do that?"

The staff in his hand suddenly glowed soft purple.

"Flame Blade. It will cut through anything. Some call them Flaming Swords. They all date to the very long ago when Zanta the Clever discovered a way to make them."

He stepped to her side. "Don't be frightened. Jonathon will carry you and then return and take the Furleen." He stepped to the opening, leaned forward. The dark wings popped out as he toppled forward and coasted away, wings beating. Then he soared up and around, headed for the roof garden.

She gasped. How could he do something like that? Then she jerked back, stifling her scream.

A gigantic shape coasted close to the window, twice as big as Yallan, great bat-shaped wings spread wide. It was the worst thing from any number of horror films that she had seen with her friends from school.

"Just me," said the monster. "Jonathon. This is our house skill form. Don't be frightened." He laughed. "I really scared Dee the first time she saw me this way.""

Sandrel stepped into the large opening in the wall.

Large arms reached forward as he drifted right up to her

and plucked her off the wall segment.

Cradling her in his arms he floated outward and then up and around, great wings beating slow.

"Purr Cat knows to wait," he told her. "Dee is here."

He canted forward and floated over the tree tops and down into a space next to a number of large vehicles, the ones that had brought the Seventh Stand to his place.

He set her next to Dee and leaped up, wings beating as he headed back over the trees to retrieve the Furleen.

Dee folded Sandrel in her arms. "You're safe now."

"I knew you would find me," Sandrel mumbled against Dee's chest.

"Lots of The People helped find you."

Sandrel leaned back. "They did?"

"Yes. Your father and Charles know many who were willing to help find you. Ralph owes debt to those ones."

"Dee?"

"Ummmmmm." Dee unscrewed a container of coffee and filled two cups, handing one to Sandrel, closing the container, and taking a sip.

"I heard them talking about two of their members being killed in the elevator. Did you do that?"

Dee took a sip. "No. I suspect that was Purr Cat. She waited for the elevator to open so she could come up."

Dee sat on the grass. "We will not be here much longer."

The great bat thing settled to the ground and set the Furleen down. Then it seemed to collapse into itself and became Jonathon.

Dee opened the container and poured Jonathon a cup of coffee and handed it up to him.

He sat next to her. Purr Cat had sat by her other side.

They waited.

Finally dark figures began to float over the tree line and settle nearby, wings disappearing as they did. Many were carrying bundles in their arms, one hand holding their staffs.

Kitea, First Hand of the Seventh Stand walked over and bowed to Dee and then to Jonathon. "We are done."

Dee stood and bowed to her. "Have them get into those vehicles. We have to wait for Ralph and Charles to return. They went to the parking structures to talk with Randy who had placed groups of his folk at each tunnel mouth to prevent escapes."

Sandrel looked at Dee.

"I will tell you the History of The Fontala later," replied Dee to the unspoken question.

She sat again and frowned into the darkness. Ralph would have to tell her who was responsible for this. He had told her that those not nice ones in this structure had been hired.

Washington, D.C.

Charles sat at his desk reading reports, something that happened every morning. He saw this as "shuffling paper," an activity which he truly disliked but realized was necessary.

He was close to the bottom of the pile when his door flew open and Randy stalked in, a newspaper clenched in one hand.

Charles waggled one hand. "Have some coffee, Randy." He smiled at his very agitated colleague. "What's up?"

Randy plopped into a chair and filled a cup from the container and took a cautious sip. He was never sure what variety of coffee Charles would be drinking, some of which he felt was pretty bad. This time it was all right.

"We, me and my teams, had that place bottled up from noon until you told us that Ralph's daughter had been rescued."

"Yep." Charles refilled his cup and leaned back.

"The only one of that crew that we bagged was one guy, a rather young member of that organization. He was running, not walking, down the tunnel to the loading dock when we grabbed him."

"Uh huh." Charles took a swallow, leaned forward and refilled his cup.

"He told us that Sandrel suggested that he ought to leave. Because he had been kind."

"O.K."

"That was three days ago."

"Yep."

Randy flattened the newspaper over Charles desk, over the reports and all.

"This article, in today's paper, says that it took the cops and the fire department several hours to cut open a number of security doors to get to the top floor after residents had reported bad smells coming down from up there."

"Uh huh."

"That place was a mess. We already read all their reports, fire and police. No survivors. The place was trashed. No papers in any desk, etc. Computers gone."

Randy stared at Charles. "This is the same thing as we found at William Williams the Third's so-called secret installation."

Charles sat up. "And?"

"There was a bedroom up there where we think Sandrel was held. The window and a piece of the wall holding that window were cut away. The same type of damage that we saw in Williams' place."

"O.K."

"So, tell me Charles, how did you get Ralph's daughter out of there?"

Charles shrugged.

"WHAT!"

"I don't know." He smiled. "Ralph said that in this case it was something that he was not going to discuss . . . with anyone."

"CRAP! Crap . . . crap . . . crap . . . crap!"

"Have some more coffee Randy."

Randy did and leaned forward and glared at Charles.

"Ummmm," said Charles.

"We were not involved in what ever happened to the Williams' installation but we were in this operation. The damage was the same. How come?"

Charles shrugged. "It is a mystery, all right."

Randy stood and set his cup on Charles' desk's corner. And stomped toward the door. "I am going to talk with Ralph!"

"Have fun."

The door slammed shut.

Timothy Grimble sat at his desk and stared at the newspaper that he held. It was the same issue that Randy had left on Charles desk.

He read it again and still found it hard to believe. From what the newspaper reporter could find out, he felt that it was some form of gang violence, an argument over territory or some such thing. That was the gist of the article.

Timothy wondered what sort of idiotic things that group had been up to. He sighed. All they had to do was one rather simple thing but apparently had poked their noses into something else, some very lethal something else.

He stood and began to walk back and forth in his office.

There had been no mention of a young woman in all that carnage. That must mean that in some way, totally not seen by the investigators of the crime scene, Ralph had taken his daughter from that group. Now that was something to think about.

In all the time he had spent inside the government he had never heard anything that would have suggested that. Ralph was just the head of something called The Council which appeared to operate as some sort of advisory thing to the President, and only the President. It didn't seem possible that such a advisory group could get the President to send in a Special Forces team to get his daughter back. If he did, the politics of that would be national news in short order.

Timothy strode up to the window behind his desk and stared out at the neatly mown grass. It must have been as reported, some sort of struggle between criminal groups. And, somehow, Ralph had snatched his daughter free in the process.

Timothy tapped his lips with the forefinger of his right hand.

Now there was a thought. Could Ralph be connected to some criminal organization? If he was, Ralph's career would be over and done with! He would have some folk check into that.

Maryland.

Shafts of afternoon sunlight decorated the end of the kitchen and made bright squares on the floor.

Ralph and his adopted daughter, Sandrel, sat and watched his wife Sandra finishing a late breakfast.

Neither of the watchers offered to help as both knew that Sandra preferred to do the cooking by herself.

As she sampled the mixture of eggs, chopped potatoes, green chilies, onions, made a slight addition to the seasoning, and gave the contents of the large cast iron pans a last stir, the front door banged open and slammed shut.

"Oh boy, brunch," laughed Charles as he walked into the kitchen. "Ummmmm, or late breakfast?"

Ralph pulled over another chair.

Sandrel stood and fetched another large plate, added more bread to the toaster, and smiled at him as he walked into the kitchen and dropped into the appropriate chair.

The four of them put a rather large dent into the contents of the pans and eliminated most of the toast.

"So, how you doing, kiddo?" asked Charles as he took a large bite from the last piece of toast which he had coated in a thick layer of cherry jam.

"Fine," replied Sandrel, standing. Charles asked her the same question every time. "Time to take a walk." She headed for the front door followed by Shadowfog, her black German Shepherd. She bent, hooked on the leash and called, "Bye, Charles." And headed out for their walk.

"Ummmm," said Charles, holding out his cup so Sandra could refill it.

"What?" asked Ralph.

"Randy was really wound up about that newspaper article and wanted to know if I knew anything about what really happened. I told him I didn't, which was true." Charles emptied his coffee cup and held it out for a refill. Sandra filled it.

"But," added Charles, after taking a big loud slurp. "I suspect he will be asking you that same thing."

Ralph shrugged. "He will get the same response you gave him."

"Fine by me." Charles laughed. He stood. "Thanks for the eats, Sandra." And headed for the door waving one arm. "See ya, Ralph."

Ralph helped Sandra clean up the kitchen and then headed for the living room to read.

Some time later he heard the front door open and close.

Sandrel and dog joined him on the couch.

"Father?" she said.

"Oh, oh." He looked at her, marked his place in the book, and set it on a table. "What?"

She held up the newspaper that had been lying on another of the small tables. "What happen there?"

Ralph shook his head. "I am not really sure."

She frowned at him.

"But," he added, "I think that Dee was responsible."

"How could she do all that?" She frowned. "She told me that she would tell me the history of The Fontala. But she left without doing that."

Sandra joined them on the couch, giving Shadowfog a shove to make room. "Dear?"

"Oh, oh, again," he said.

"I think that Sandrel should spend the rest of the summer with Dee learning about her folk."

Ralph nodded. And smiled at his daughter.

"Think of it as a kind of summer school," he said. "Sandra is right. You were raised as one of the people and have never really learned about your mother's folk."

Sandra stood. "No time like the present." She smiled. "Shall we go?" she asked her adopted daughter.

Sandrel stood, clipped the leash on Shadowfog's collar. "She is coming with me."

"Should be all right," said Ralph. "I suspect."

Sandra nodded.

They were gone.

Ralph picked up his book and shrugged. Dee would know what Sandrel needed to know.

He might even finish this book before he was interrupted.

House Darthar Na.

Dee was sitting in one of the smaller outside rooms with the large picture windows framing the meadow and surrounding forest just beyond the entrance staircase. She was sipping from her cup and thinking of querying her daughters on their studies.

The door to the room opened and they walked in.

Dee stood and turned.

Sandra, Sandrel, and Shadowfog walked in.

"Surprise," said Sandra.

"Most so," said Dee. She filled two more cups and handed them out. And waited for them to sit before she did.

"Ummmmmm." Dee took a sip. And waited.

Sandra took a sip. And waited.

"I thought," began Sandra, "as did Ralph, that Sandrel should spent a number of months here. She needs to learn about herself and her folk. She doesn't understand what just happened, ahh, with those guys."

Dee nodded. And looked at the young woman. "Some of the training will be hard. You will learn what it is to be one of The Feyra, The Hidden Ones. You have only a tiny bit of experience with us and years of living as one of the People." She smiled. "It is about time for you to know who you really are."

Sandrel looked at Sandra.

Sandra smiled, and wiped an errant tear from her face. "It really is time, daughter mine." She stood.

Sandrel set her cup down, jumped up and hugged her.

"My daughters will help," said Dee, as the door flew open and they walked in.

"Tiela, Winala, this is Sandrel. She will be here for some months, as the People mark time, studying. You will help her understand." She looked at Sandra. "I will ask Jonathon to help also." The Ice Cats crowded into the room.

Sandra stepped back.

And was gone.

"Tiela, find Sandrel a room on the floor of The Fontala. It will good for her to see so many of her kind in one place."

As Tiela led Sandrel and Shadowfog from the room, Dee said to Sandrel, "We will talk later." Then she asked Winala how her studies were progressing.

Once Dee felt satisfied with Winala's progress, she left her daughter and climbed the stairs to the floor occupied by The Fontala.

She found Sandrel, Yallan, and Kitea in the meeting room of The Seventh Stand. Sandrel had left Shadowfog in her room. Kitea and Yallan had been telling Sandrel about The Fontala and some of their past history.

Yallan and Kitea stood and bowed to Dee.

Dee bowed in return.

"Kitea and Sandrel, come with me, please. Many thanks, Yallan."

Dee led Kitea and Sandrel down the hall and opened a door, stepped inside, and waited.

They stood on a small balcony four floors above The Training Hall's floor.

Dee pointed at the great open space. "Kitea, go fly around."

Kitea climbed over the balcony railing and stood on the narrow ledge. Her great black wings appeared as she leaned forward and coasted away, taking a great swooping path around the vast open space, her wings giving a pump now and then.

Dee climbed over the railing, stood on the narrow ledge and turned back to face Sandrel. Her great white wings appeared as she fell back and hovered there, wings beating.

"Wings are a House Darthar Na skill. White is the normal

color. I had Ar, the House Trainer, make The Seventh Stand's dark."

Dee drifted closer, floated up and over the railing and settled inside the balcony, wings disappearing. "Now you know about that and some of the history of The Fontala."

She pointed at the door. "Now we can go to your room and talk about other things."

Washington, D.C.

Charles took another of the doughnuts from the large basket, took a large bite, and chewed happily. Then he took a swallow from his coffee cup.

"We seem to be in a sort of impasse."

Ralph joined him in taking another of the doughnuts.

"Seems so," he said around a mouthful.

Charles leaned back in his chair and smiled.

"Oh," said Ralph.

"Yep." replied Charles.

"What?"

"Daniel went over there to look around. He said that he had a idea that he wanted to check on."

Ralph shrugged.

"He is really good at that sort of thing." Charles laughed. "And he volunteered!"

"Think he will be able to find out anything?"

"I gave him all the info I got from Swift. And he said something very interesting."

Ralph stared at him.

"Yah," stated Charles.

"Do I want to hear this?"

"Well, he was smiling when he said it, so I suppose it will be safe. Hope so."

"And?"

"He said that as long as he is in the know about our, ummmmm, different friends, that maybe he could find a way to find what we have been trying to find."

"Now that is to worry about."

Charles shrugged. "Worse that could happen is that he would get killed."

"No," stated Ralph.

"Huh?"

"The worse that could happen would be that group getting really getting pissed off with all of us."

"What?"

"Charles, they have houses all over the world and a very determined need to not be involved in our activities. And a strong cultural need to keep us from knowing of their existence and getting involved in their lives. If Daniel sticks his nose into their business they might decide to, ahhh, terminate our relationship with them."

Charles slumped in his chair and stared at his long time friend. "Don't tell me that we all have to find new houses to live in and all that, not again."

Ralph shook his head. "I don't think that we could hide from them if we tried." He sighed. "Sandrel is visiting with Dee and learning all about her ancestry and all that entails. Ahhhh, hopefully, Dee would say something before a bunch of agitated folk from her cultural group did anything, ahhh, too extreme."

He shrugged. "Can't worry about Daniel though. He is gone somewhere, doing something. Maybe, if we are lucky, we will find out after the fact. He could just disappear."

Charles nodded and took another doughnut. "In that case, have another." He held out the basket.

House Arilia.

First Brother, Fair Aral, strode into the room, and bowed deeply.

"Head," he said softly. "That male of the People is walking back and forth on the trail calling loudly."

Dark Sybil looked up from the book she had been reading and making notes in the margins. "What male of the People?"

"That one we healed and returned."

"Ummmmmm."

"That male yells, screams, loudly, over and over again, one word."

She stared at him.

"He cries out loudly, HELP!"

She stood. "Bring him here, willing or not. He may join me, I am hungry."

She left the room and turned down the wood paneled tunnel that carved through the solid rock of the mountain toward the appropriate room. What could that one want coming here like that? Perhaps all that care they gave that one was a waste after all.

House Darthar Na.

Dee and Sandrel stood in the middle of the training hall, a great open space whose ceiling was a number of floors above their head. A short figure stood in front of them. He wore clothes of a soft blue color that complimented his blue skin tones.

"This is Ar, The House Trainer. Every house has one. A house trainer knows all the house skills of their house."

He bowed to Sandrel.

"I am Ar'ga'da'fazza'din'ban'ahm'na. I am also Princess Daliera's Advisor and Teacher as well as the one that trains all those that the House Head believes should be trained. Do call me

Ar." He smiled, and waved a hand of rather long fingers at the great open space. "This is the Training Hall. It is well guarded. Nothing cast in here may penetrate the walls, floor, or ceiling and affect anyone outside. At times the doors are locked to prevent accidental, eh, problems."

"I wish her to be trained in push," said Dee. "She needs to be able to defend herself."

Ar bowed. "As the Head wishes."

Sandrel looked at Dee. "Push?"

Dee nodded. "Ready Ar?"

"Of course," he stated. "I am always ready. Princess."

Dee shoved her hand at him, palm out.

Ar flew back and tumbled across the floor. He stood and walked back and smiled, sharp teeth glistening in the light. "Have no fear, ummmmm, Sandrel. I am unharmed."

"Sandrel," explained Dee, "is the First Daughter and only surviving offspring of House Kaanatan. Her house has skills that focus primarily on three dimensional art. She has been raised as one of the People and is the adopted daughter of House Sextet. That people house, the only one of its kind, is an Adopted House to House Darthar Na."

Ar bowed. And looked at Sandrel. "It is hard work to learn one of the house skills that is not of your house."

Sandrel bowed back. "Shall we start?"

Dee smiled at Ar. "Do your best.

Ar huffed, just a little. "I always do my best. Princess."

"I know you do." She nodded to Sandrel. "Ar will tell me when you are done practicing."

She walked from the hall and heard the door lock itself.

House Darthar.

Jonathon and Hofga sat in one of the small, comfortable

rooms, sipping from their cups and watching what the watch thing rented from Hondo the Thing Dealer was seeing. They sat in comfortable chairs with small tables close by to set their cups on, if they wished. Light wood paneling on the wall and a large window with a pleasant view added to the relaxed feeling of the room.

Hofga pointed out that the tall, conical hill standing in isolation, had been somewhat flat on top before it had been altered. He could read the rock and the structure of the environment as easy as Jonathon could read a book. It was a house skill.

"It appears," added Hofga, "that the structure on the top was constructed from the stone of the hill's core in the not very long ago, but long ago as the People measure time."

Jonathon nodded. "That not very nice People cluster seem to have taken up residence there from the recent look of the repair."

"And they still keep that young female captive. The People do act very strange." He held out his cup. Jonathon refilled it and then his own.

Hofga took a sip. "Think that we should ask Dee about this? She showed that portrait of the young female to one of the People and he got very excited for some reason."

"Ummmmmm." Jonathon took a sip.

Hofga took a sip and waited.

"Perhaps we should." Jonathon nodded.

House Arilia.

Dark Sybil looked up from the book she had been reading and glared at him, that male of the People, as the pair entered the room.

"Why do you come to bother us, Daniel Fanzle?"

Fair Aral backed up to the wall and guarded himself. She had a very dangerous look to her face.

Daniel bowed to her. "I am very sorry about that but I have a great, umm, need for help with a bad problem and I think that, perhaps, you might be able to aid me. I had no-one else to ask."

He bowed again. And waited.

She stood, nodded to him, and walked over to a table and filled three cups with coffee. She handed on to Fair Aral, one to Daniel, took the last, sat back in her chair at the small table, and sipped. And waited.

Daniel, who had been tutored by Dee in the appropriate Feyra etiquette sat, took a sip, and waited.

Fair Arla did the same, but sat where he could watch Daniel carefully.

"Ummmmmmm." Dark Sybil took a sip.

"Every house has unique house skills," Daniel began. "You healed me and in some manner got me back into my residence without anyone knowing that you did." He took a sip. And waited.

"Most so." Dark Sybil took a sip.

"A, ahh, cluster of very not nice People took a young woman from her, ahh, family. Her family is very bothered by this and has been trying for some time to find where she is being held." He took a sip.

She nodded. "Why should we be concerned with the very strange behavior of some very not nice People? We do not wish to involve ourselves with People behavior. We do not wish to have People become aware of our existence."

He nodded. And took a sip. "I know of your existence."

Dark Sybil stared at Daniel. "Perhaps we made a mistake."

Daniel jerked. He took a sip and held out his cup. She

refilled it.

"Perhaps so," he said. "But!"

"Ummmmmmm." She leaned back in her chair and refilled her cup and looked at Fair Aral, who shook his head.

"Ralph Fredrickson is the Head of the only People House in existence, House Sextet. It was created at the direction of Daliera Fontala, Head, House Darthar Na. House Sextet is an adopted house to House Darthar Na and bound by all the Feyra obligations. I am now an adopted member of House Sextet."

Fair Arla jumped to his feet. And quickly sat down.

Dark Sybil stared at Daniel, eyes wide. "True?"

"Most so." Daniel had adopted some of Dee's dialect as well.

She took a sip. "This was unknown to us."

"It is a House Darthar Na secret known to a few."

"Ummmmmmm."

"The same People male that is responsible for having those very not nice ones take that young female is also responsible for having another, ah, cluster of very not nice ones take House Sextet Head Ralph's adopted daughter Sandrel, a Feyra."

Fair Arla leaped up, snarling. "Those very not nice ones must pay the price!"

Daniel nodded and took a sip. "In that case they did. Daliera rescued Sandrel with the help of Ralph and his, umm, associates."

"Ummmmm." Dark Sybil took a sip and nodded at Fair Arla who sat down. "It would seem that this House Sextet owes House Darthar Na great debt."

"Most so," replied Daniel. "Because you healed me and I realized who you were, I am now adopted into House Sextet and thus bound by all the obligations of house to house. I spent some time in House Darthar Na learning, ah, as much as one of the

People can, that is."

Dark Sybil nodded. And stood. "I am still hungry. Will you join Fair Arla and me?"

Daniel stood and bowed to her. "Most kind."

"You may tell me of this other matter as we eat. Then Fair Arla and I will speak on that."

House Darthar Na.

Dee and her daughters, Tiela and Winala, accompanied by the Ice Cats, one pet for each daughter, sat in one of the dining rooms. The Ice Cats were very well behaved. They sat very still next to their adopted daughter. But they watched the food very carefully. Dinner had just started when the door to the room opened and Sandrel stumbled in.

Sandrel was sweat stained and covered with patches of wet. She was smiling as she crashed down into a chair.

Dee handed her a cup of coffee.

"It worked." laughed Sandrel.

"Ummmmm." Dee spooned some food onto Sandrel's plate.

"I pushed Ar. He was standing about two arm's length way." She laughed. "He really flew backward!"

Dee smiled at her.

Tiela and Winala laughed with Sandrel. They remembered when they had first mastered that house skill. It was the first one taught.

"Tomorrow you can start reading a number of books in the library." Dee refilled various cups that required filling. "They will help you understand our culture. Our culture and your culture."

Sandrel dumped more food onto her plate. "Really worked up an appetite." She looked at Dee. "There is so much to know."

Dee nodded. "I know. But you are starting at a much younger age than I did."

Sandrel nodded, her mouth full.

Dee took a sip. "Ummmmmm."

"What?" Sandrel swallowed, looked at Dee.

"What you learn is not to talked about with any of the People, not all. We do not do that! Not even to Ralph or Sandra!"

Sandrel nodded.

House Darthar.

Jonathon and Hofga sat in one of the small, comfortable rooms, sipping from their cups. They sat in comfortable chairs with small tables close by to set their cup on, if they wished. Light wood paneling on the wall and a large window with a pleasant view added to the relaxed feeling of the room.

Dee walked into the room. "Jonathon?"

He filled a cup and handed it to her, then sat back down.

She sat and took a sip. And waited.

"Ummmmm."

"What?" she asked. "Why did you bring me here?"

"I want to you look at what the watch thing is seeing."

Dee nodded. And took a sip. "O.K."

Jonathon stared at her. At times her people dialect was puzzling.

Dee suppressed her smile. "Yes. I will watch it." She nodded.

And they all did.

Jonathon took a sip.

"Is that the same young People female?" he asked.

"Yes."

"Ummmm."

" You were there when I had a drawing made and showed

it to Daniel who got very excited about it."

"Do you know why?"

"No. Just more strange People behavior I guess. But it is the same young female."

A thing flew into the room from somewhere. It looked like bird turned into a bat, more or less. It was soft green with bright blue eyes. It perched on Hofga's leg and peered up at him.

"It is a messenger from House Arilia," explained Hofga. "What do you want, this time?" he asked. Then he nodded.

He frowned at something and then looked a Jonathon.

"Ummmmmm." Jonathon took a sip. And waited.

"Dark Sybil wishes you to call her and her, ah, guest here. To talk."

Jonathon nodded. And did.

Dark Sybil and Daniel walked into the room.

Dark Sybil bowed. Daniel hastily did the same thing.

Jonathon filled two cups and handed them around. And sat and took a sip.

The pair sat, took sips, and waited.

"Ummmmm," said Jonathon.

Dark Sybil nodded, took a sip.

"This male has things to tell you." She looked from Hofga to Jonathon to Dee. "Perhaps there is a thing that we should be concerned about."

Daniel took a sip and began to explain.

When he finished, Dee stared at him. "Are you saying that the same People male is responsible for having Sandrel taken and that other female?"

Daniel nodded. "His actions are very bothering to, ah, House Sextet, as well as to a very powerful People family. Ralph is working very hard to try and find that young, um, female and reunite her with her family. It is a, umm, obligation that he has."

Dee nodded. And took a sip.

"Do you know the name of this male that causes all the bother?"

Daniel nodded.

"Tell me that name!" snapped Dee.

Daniel jerked back in his chair.

Dee stood and glared at him. "DO IT!" And waved a hand at Hofga and Jonathon, warning them away.

"AHHHHH dota!" grumbled Hofga.

Dark Sybil watched Dee very carefully.

Jonathon took a sip and refilled Hofga's cup.

Daniel swallowed hard. "His name is Timothy Grimble."

Dee nodded and turned toward the door. Sandra walked in. "Dee?"

"Come with me." Dee herded Sandra into the hallway and told where she wanted to go.

Inside the room Daniel looked from face to face.

"What is she going to do?" he asked.

Jonathon shrugged.

Hofga took a sip and then another.

Dark Sybil nodded.

"What?" asked Daniel.

Into The Woods. Or Something Like That.

Dee and Sandra looked at it. It was a hole. In a cliff. High on a mountain side. They had come here following Dee's directions.

The cliff stretched dark grey and light grey bands far to either side. There was only the one hole. Here and there, crooked and warped vegetation clung to small crevices making small green spots on all those grey tones.

Dee pointed at the tunnel. "I will enter. Stay out here,

Sandra. It will be safe."

She walked deep inside the tunnel. This was something that she didn't want Sandra to know about. When she was finished, they would go back.

The walls glowed dull green light. She turned a bend and stopped. At the door in the wall. And knocked.

"Kakmir!" growled something, somewhere. That told Dee that the one she wanted to visit was at home.

She thumped on the door. "Open! Dee, come to visit!"

"Do dak gar pit zik! Piz zik!"

"SILENCE!" roared someone as the door creaked inward. A short, rather globular figure stood there, peering out, all of four feet tall, wearing a bright yellow something or other, which appeared most like a tent turned into a garment.

"Ah hum. Do come in." The speaker backed up, and turned, speaking to her as he wobbled down the tunnel. "Don't mind the door thing. Still in training. I remember you."

"Strange, strange, strange, strange," mumbled Dee as she always did to herself as she followed him, or it, or whatever. It was just as she remembered when she had last visited here. Hondo never changes, it appeared.

Her host dropped into a chair set next to a table and waggled an appendage at the other chairs. As soon as she sat, a mug was shoved at her.

She picked up her mug and took the tiniest of sips. And held the liquid in one cheek. She knew better than to drink it. The stuff was a disaster. For her stomach.

Hondo took a great swallow. "GOOD! GOOD! DRINK!"

The stuff smelled awful, gut wrenching horrible.

"I want to rent a thing, a, ah ummmm, special thing."

"We try harder!" Hondo banged his mug on the table. "Always." Dee took a tiny sip and added it to the little already held in her cheek. He refilled his mug and eyed her's.

Then she told Hondo what she wished, and why, and asked if he could do that.

Hondo nodded. "A very not nice one!"

She nodded. "This has to be a secret."

"SECRET!" bellowed Hondo. "Big, dark secret."

She handed him a sheet of paper and then another with carefully written instructions on it.

"Great debt is owed."

"A deal!" Hondo settled somewhat lower in his chair. "But no tell, ever."

"Absolutely," agreed Dee.

Dee stood, and bowed. She hurried from the room and down the long hall, tunnel, and outside.

She walked quickly to the nearby meadow, spun away and decorated a handy shrub with Hondo's drink. "Horrible. Ghastly."

She wiped her mouth on her sleeve. "Take me back to Jonathon's, Sandra."

House Darthar.

Jonathon looked up as the door to the room opened where he and Hofga, Dark Sybil, and Daniel were sitting and watched the pair walk in.

Sandra looked at Dee. "Am I done?"

"Most so."

Sandra disappeared.

Jonathon stood and filled cups and handed them around, then he refilled his and Hofga's and sat down.

"Ummmmm." Jonathon took a sip and waited.

The rest sat down and did the same thing.

"I asked Astal of House Patelon to, once again, help us."

Dee took a sip. "And Armilin of The Fontala to come as well to give advice."

Jonathon nodded.

"I would like Astal to see what the watch thing sees and I would like you, Jonathon, or Hofga to tell it when to change position as Astal requires. She is going to draw a very detailed view and map of that hilltop structure so we, all of us, can make a plan on how to free that female of the People."

Dee stood and bowed to them all, deeply. "Shall we start?" She sat and took a sip.

Virginia.

The large pickup parked behind one of the many police cars that crowded along the curb in front of the large and sprawling ranch-style house in an area of large and sprawling and very expensive ranch-style houses. In the driveway an ambulance was backed up with the rear doors swung wide. Uniformed police stood in small clusters here and there as well as others dressed in suits.

Charles jumped from the driver's seat and walked to the front of the truck to wait for Ralph to join him.

They strolled over to where the front door into the house had been. Standing back, they could see a number of investigators slowly crawling amidst the debris picking up this or that piece and sealing them in evidence bags.

One of them looked up. "You'll have go around and come in the back door."

"What happened here?" asked Charles.

The man shrugged. "Something blew the door, door jamb, and sections of the attached wall into the far wall and all the furniture, mostly demolishing the furniture, as you can see. So far we haven't found any trace of explosive, or anything else, to explain what did it." He went back to work.

Charles shrugged and headed back to the rear of the building, Ralph walking at his side.

They stopped at the back door and signed the clipboard held by the policewoman manning the door and controlling the flow of personnel in and out of the crime scene.

She glanced down to see who these guys were. Then she stared at Ralph. "The White House? You guys again?"

He nodded and smiled at her as they stepped past.

She pointed, told them to go down the hall, to the second bedroom where they should be able to hear the voices.

As they walked down the hall, they heard her mumble about politicians messing things up.

At the door to the second bedroom, they stopped and peered inside.

The large man in the rumpled suit turned and stared at them. "I am Detective Ransom. I remember you guys! Stay out of here!"

Charles flipped open a thin leather case as did Ralph.

Ransom stepped close enough to read. "And why are you here? This time?"

Ralph smiled. "We are the ones who had been investigating Timothy Grimble for a numbers of crimes. Where is he?"

The Detective laughed, a hollow sound. "Step just inside the door, no further."

As they did they could see blood on the floor, on the walls, and splattered across the ceiling.

Both looked around the room for the body.

Charles frowned.

Ralph looked at Detective Ransom.

The Detective waved one hand at the room.

"Where is Grimble? Everywhere, he is everywhere."

"What happened? Here?" Ralph's eyes searched the room for the body or body parts.

Ransom shrugged. "Haven't the foggiest idea. But you two and I know that we have seen something like this before." He stepped closer to them. "You guys have any ideas you want to share? This is the same as the last time I saw you two. How come?"

"No idea," said Charles. "We just wanted to see what had happened to our bad guy."

Ransom stared at Ralph. "You taking over this case? You can have it, if you want it. I will be glad to get rid of it."

"No." Ralph shook his head. "Let's go, Charles." He nodded at Ransom. "Best of luck."

Ransom laughed as they headed back down the hall. And called after them. "I am going to reread everything of that other case. Nothing like this happens twice and is not related!"

They were driving down the main road, the one they had come by, when Ralph reached over and poked Charles on the shoulder.

"What is going on?"

"As Detective Ransom said, no idea."

Rugged and Isolated.

In this region of rugged terrain they had found and bought it. It was an up thrusting conical hill, more than hill, less than mountain, standing by itself. A narrow path crawled in a spiral up the steep slope to the summit to where the real prize sat.

An ancient stone structure encased the top. It had obviously been placed to watch over the surrounding land. Batu had inspected it and found that, much to his surprise, that they could easily repair the roofs and in a relatively short time bring the place up to minimal standards, sufficient to suit their needs.

Tonight the clouds hung low almost brushing across the tallest towers of the structure. The late night faint light from the sliver of the moon barely penetrated that thick layer. The structure was dark and shrouded in deep shadows.

Two members of The Golden Cartouche sat on folding chairs just outside the entryway and stared down the narrow path into the night. It was a very dull thing to do, but all took turns doing it, just in case someone should dare make their way up the narrow trail the circled the steep slopes from the base of the hill near mountain to the entryway.

Suddenly the pair were yanked from their chairs as great clawed paws wrapped around their heads and tumbled the bodies down the trail. The two Furleen slipped on silent soft paws into the courtyard and sat on either side of the main door to the structure. They faded into the stone. And waited.

Arliana lay on her bed, under her single blanket, and talked ever so softly to the one of her captors that she called "The Polite One."

The bedroom had a small skylight and a smaller window located down low on the outside wall. Through that window she could see part of the inner courtyard during the day. Late at night it was mostly shadow.

The Polite One sat in the very rickety rocking chair, the only piece of furniture in the room other than the bed. He slipped into her room, always very late at night, when the bulk of his group were sound asleep. He had told her that it was a good way to look at the stars. On a clear night, which was most of the time, it reminded him of home. He was mostly quiet. But, sometimes, they talked, a little, in soft voices so no-one outside the room could hear.

"Very low and thick clouds," he murmured.

"There is always tomorrow night," she suggested.

Suddenly he gasped and slipped to his knees, arms crossed over his chest, and sighed, a long, protracted sigh.

"We are doomed," he wept.

"What?" Arliana sat up and tossed the blanket aside. She was dressed in her clothes. She was always dressed in her clothes. She had no option.

"We must have done something terrible, terrible, terrible," he sobbed.

"What are you talking about?" she whispered, afraid that he would wake some of the others and get them both in trouble. "Shhhhhhhh!"

He pointed upward with one quivering arm, finger extended. "I saw them!" he hissed. "The Dark Angels."

She leaped to her feet and stared up through the skylight. "I don't see anything."

He stood and grabbed her arm. "I will help you flee this place. Come!" He tugged her toward the door, fumbled with the key, and finally unlocked and slowly pushed open the door.

He led her down the stairs. "Quiet, quiet," he murmured. "The Dark Angels come to those that have done something terrible. All know this!"

He led her along the main hall and to the outside door. Ever so slowly he pulled it open and peered out into the gloom of the inner courtyard.

"Now," he whispered, "we have to get past the two that guard the entry. Stay right behind me."

Ever so slowly they crept to the entryway.

"Gone," he gasped as he stared at the folding chairs lying on their sides. He spun and pushed his face close to her's. "It is as

I said. They have been taken by The Dark Angels."

He pointed down the narrow path. "Go that way, do not stop. Maybe they won't come after you."

Arliana glanced around and then down the narrow trail. Well, she thought, if I go slow I probably won't slip and fall all the way down. She started forward.

And took exactly two steps.

Some thing grabbed her by the forearms and held her tight, pressing again her back. "Don't scream, they will hear you!"

"Who . . . who . . . who . . . are you?"

"Your rescuers. We are going to get you back to your father. Soooo, no noise, not a peep. O.K.?"

"Sure," she whispered, hoping that it was really true.

She tried to turn her head to look at her new captor. "Where's The Polite One?"

"Who?"

"That guy that was with me."

"He has been taken."

"Don't hurt him, please."

He sighed. At least to Arliana it sounded like a man.

"Stand right here, I'll be right back." She turned and watched a figure dressed in dark clothes run back into the inner courtyard.

She waited in the silence.

Then she saw him returning, pulling someone by the arm. "This the guy?"

"Yes." The Polite One had a bag over his head.

She reached out and held one of his hands. "You'll be all right," she said to him. Then she asked the other, "Won't he?"

"If you wish." The man stepped closer. "We need to go down the trail now. We don't want to get caught in the middle."

She turned and tugged gently at the hand she held. "Come on, we will walk very slowly down the hill." The other followed them as they did.

Numbers of silent figures dressed in black ran up the hill past them. They all carried long staffs that glowed with a faint purple glow. Not one made a sound as they ran.

The Free Floating Mind.

Dee, Janice, and Sandrel had been on a book tour, wandering across the United States from large book store to large book store. It was the standard route, established some time ago by Janice and agreed to by Dee's publisher. Janice carried a company credit card and a zippered small case stuffed with expense money. The case of money had been agreed to by Dee's publisher at Dee's insistence and after much grumbling by the head man who had stared at her and wondered why all authors were that way, beyond understanding.

Now Dee, Janice, and Sandrel were at the end of the big store tour. This was the last stop.

Dee and Sandrel sat on the small platform on the hard chairs, the hard-backed folding chairs, and watched the people settling down in the rows of similar marginally comfortable folding chairs. Dee leaned sideways and said, "Hold this for me while I do the author show-and-tell stuff."

Sandrel took the staff and looked at Dee, "Why are you carrying this thing around?"

"Daniel gave it to me. He said that it was a souvenir. When I get home I will hang in on a wall in the main hall."

Janice stood in the back and talked with the store employees. Dee took a sip from the tall paper cup of coffee with the paper insulating sleeve slipped around it. And waited.

A tall somewhat slender man, dressed in a pastel pink

colored shirt and trousers stepped up to the small podium and cleared his throat.

"Welcome," he began, and waited for them to quiet down. "Welcome to the Free Floating Mind Bookstore and tonight's event. Our guest authors are made up of one you all know and have read and enjoyed and her new co-author. Tonight Dee will answer questions first and then read some of the first two chapters of their co-authored new novel which continues the on-going saga of those new and unusual characters that came into existence in that new fantasy genre all Dee's own. As it stated on the dust jacket, she and her co-author wrote this while they were working on a special project, meeting new people, and finding new inspiration."

He laughed. "But here she is, back and well-rested, and ready to read and discuss the fourth volume with her new writing partner. Please warmly welcome tonight's guests, D. Grant and Ms. Sandrel Fredrickson!"

In the midst of the applause, Dee stepped up to the small podium, shook his hand, and took a sip from her cup, and waited.

Finally she held out her free hand, and smiled at them. "Questions? Before I read?"

Hands shot up.

She pointed at a young woman.

"Miss Grant, why are you and your co-author the damsels in distress in your new book?"

Dee laughed. "All my other books have had one so I thought it might be fun, and interesting, then, to be one in my own story." She sipped. "After all, it is more interesting to see my book from the inside out, so to speak. Now there are two of us." She laughed.

A man waved his hand. "Aren't your main characters

rather hard on the vampire and similar literature as it is being written today? Or yesterday?"

Dee nodded. "I suppose." She grinned. "But then, that is just the way that they see things." She winked at the questioner.

And so it went until she halted them so she could start the last part of the evening's presentation. She thought to herself, it really was fun being an author.

She took a sip, cleared her throat, and began to read.

"Stirrings . . . New Mexico . . . The gentle breeze drifted lazy . . ."

People sat back and relaxed into the story.

New Mexico.

Daniel Fanzle had been drifting from art gallery to art gallery around the immediate area. Santa Fe had many such places. Sometimes he bought a piece of art that appealed to him, but mostly he just looked. It was a relaxing activity and it gave him time to ponder whatever he might want to think about.

Now, mid-morning of the next day, Daniel, after a leisurely breakfast at one of his favorite establishments, was once again drifting from art gallery to art gallery. He was puzzling over a stray bit of information that he had read. His staff had seen it and had made sure that he received it. But at the moment, that was of a lower importance on his mental list of things to think about.

And so, as he drifted from here to there and then somewhere else, he thought about all the things that had happened to him over the recent past and sighed. Other than a very few people, he really had no-one that he could talk to, and discuss honestly, about the truly different. During his previous career he had seen lots of strange things and behavior but nothing that measured up to what he now knew was out there.

He only knew where one group lived but he doubted that they would be very understanding if he just turned up for a visit to talk about things.

Perhaps his best choice was to visit with Ralph and Sandra.

The Three Villages.

The three villages were strung along the one-lane, dirt rut that passed as the road. The highest village, at the end of the not very wide valley was slightly more populated than the other two. Hence it was regarded as the social and cultural center of the meager population of the valley.

The folk here, in this mountainous region of eastern Europe were isolated, both in terms of their environmental setting and in terms of their attitudes. They had a low regard for "outsiders," those that did not share their cultural values and remembered, such as it might have been, history.

He walked along the dusty road that was mostly a trail and walked to the door of one of the small houses and pushed it open and stepped inside. It was his home.

Two days latter everyone gathered in the upper village in the big barn, the only structure large enough to hold them all. He handed the leader of the villages a large briefcase. It was full of money.

Then he explained that no more would be coming from the outside. He told them of all their successes and then of the night when the Dark Angels came. Men gasped and women wailed. He stated that it was Dark Angels because he had seen the figure dressed in black floating from the heavens on great black wings. Everyone wanted to know which of the many powerful deities he and the others had angered.

He explained that he had no idea. He was the lowest member of their group, the one that was told the least and ordered around the most. Then he told of the prisoner that saved his life and how he had come by such a large quantity of money.

He shook his head. No, he didn't know who she was. He really had no idea, only that the group expected to be paid a very large sum when they turned her over to the one that had issued the contract. This was also a secret held only by their leader.

Finally he sat in a wooden chair and stated that from this time on he was going to be a farmer, never anything else.

And that is what he did. But folk began calling him "The Polite One" because he had told them about that.

Washington, D.C.

Ralph and Daniel strolled down the hallway, dressed in dark blue suits, very expensive, neatly tailored, matching dark blue shirts, red ties, passing offices that were mostly quiet in this early part of the evening. Now and then Ralph waved and smiled at the few hard workers that were finishing up in order to be ready for the next morning's burst of activity and meetings that were the normal part of doing business here in the center of the nation's government.

Then they stopped outside one of the doors, opened it and walked into an office suite, once a private domain, not empty expect for a very sad-faced secretary who was slowly packing personal things in boxes and setting papers and files for the FBI to inspect as they investigated the death of Timothy Grimble.

"Is there anything that I can do?" asked Ralph.

She looked up, wiped a tear away, and shook her head.

"No, I don't think so. It was terrible news." She turned back to what she was doing.

Ralph backed into the hall, gesturing Daniel to come along.

As the door closed, Daniel asked, "What am I doing here?" He plucked at his attire. "In this getup? I never dress this way."

Ralph pointed down the hall at one of the doors. "Going to see him."

Daniel stared at Ralph. "The President? Why does he want to see me?" He could think of any number of things that The President could do to him for certain activities he had been engaged in, in the past.

Ralph tugged him into motion. "He just wants to thank you for leading his daughter down and away from that place."

"Oh."

"You want to tell me how you came to do that and who helped you?"

Daniel shook his head. "Promised that I wouldn't."

"O.K."

Ralph stopped at the door and then opened it and led Daniel inside, saying, "Mr. President, may I introduce Daniel Fanzle. You wished to see him."

The door closed behind them.

Just Another Small Town.

This was their last stop after wandering the United States, popping into a number of the larger urban areas, visiting the bookstores. It was a book tour for her new book, just as she had promised her publisher. The pair of them, the authors, and their tour organizer, had gotten, again, some small amount of tired from answering the same old questions, asked over and over and over again. It was interesting in a strange sort of a way. But tiring. As it always was.

Dee had suggested to Janice, once again, that maybe they could just create a handout with those same questions and the usual answers printed on it. That way, she hoped, someone would ask something new. Her companion had argued that it wasn't a good idea and she had agreed. Once again.

Finally, they were visiting some of the small towns and their bookstores, often the only bookstore, and giving the stores and whoever might be there more of an unprepared show and tell than the usual thing that they did. It was fun to be spontaneous and relaxed rather than programmed.

Now, here they were, three females, Dee, Janice, and Sandrel, in a small town in one of the western states, well off the main road, having a meal in the only restaurant. This small town had become one of the favorite places for Dee and Janice to visit. Dee had made Sandrel her co-author on this book and was showing her exactly what an author really did other than writing.

"Still much better than the usual hotel restaurant stuff." Dee licked the frosting off her lips and smiled at her traveling companions. "Much better."

Sandrel smiled at her.

Janice nodded. "I agree. Here we are again, out here in the middle of nowhere again. In this town again." She laughed.

Dee smiled. "All those big urban book stores look alike. Out here I can see open spaces, talk with a few people at a time, listen to the quiet, and begin to think,ummm ah, about our new novel, Sandrel and I." She laughed. "So when you call the publisher again, you can tell him that. It will make him happy."

She waved at the only waitress, who strolled over, and looked down at her. "Somethin?"

"Yes. I would like another piece of that pie. And more coffee, please." She looked across the table.

"Just coffee, please." said Janice. Sandrel ordered more pie, and a cup of tea, an unusual beverage for one of The Feyra. She had developed a taste for it from living with her adopted parents, Ralph and Sandra.

The waitress shuffled over to the pie case, a circular pie container with a number of shelves inside a clear plastic shell, cut chunks from the appropriate pie, slid them onto plates, and returned, and set them on the table.

"Here ya go, Dears. Coffee is just finished. I'll bring you a pot." She winked. "I do enjoy seeing someone who enjoys what we fix. I remember you." She smiled at Dee and Janice. "Welcome back." She wandered away, came back, refilled two coffee cups, added more hot water to Sandrel's tea pot, and headed into the back to talk with the cook. And make a few phone calls.

Dee smiled and cut a big chunk off the slice with her fork. "Nice country. Lots of open space and mountains. And good pie."

"When you two are done, let's just take another stroll around for awhile. We can cruise the main drag, such as it is. See if anything has changed. See how your number one fans are doing." Janice laughed. Sandrel looked at her, wondering what they were doing in this town, exactly.

"Sure," said Dee. She took a big bite and then a sip of coffee.

"Ah ummmmmm." Dee finished her dessert and sipped at her coffee.

As soon as they were ready, Dee paid the bill, left a generous tip, and walked outside.

Janice pointed. "As I remember, the edge of town is over there."

They strolled that way in the gathering dusk. And as they wandered down the sidewalk the sky darkened and the few street lights came on. They heard no traffic or any other sounds. It was still a very quiet town.

"Still quite a small place," said Dee. They had hit the edge of town. So they turned and wandered back toward the other edge of town.

"Certainly is," agreed Janice, pointing, as they entered the marginal downtown area. "With one not too bad motel, one pretty good restaurant, the one and only bar in town with a rather unkempt exterior and a somewhat brand new large window, still washed and clean, and that little bookstore over there which seems to be still in business."

They walked over to the bookstore and reintroduced themselves to the owner and the few customers checking the selection.

Then they talked, the authors and the few customers, about the usual things. Dee smiled to see that her books were still on display as well as the new one by her and Sandrel. "Thanks," she said to the owner.

Then they walked in, seeming to fill the available space in the front of the store. Two very large, in several directions, men, stopped, and stared at them. One mouth dropped open. Both men were wearing heavy, badly worn work boots, dirty denim jeans and denim jackets over faded shirts of some barely visible pattern. Both stomachs were threatening to overflow wide leather belts.

One stepped close to Dee and looked down at her.

"My, my, my," he rumbled.

"Good to see you again," rumbled the other. "Right, Little Fred?"

Sandrel looked up and stared at them and wondered whether she would have to defend Dee.

Little held out a well thumbed book. "Ahhhh, Ms. Grant and, uh, Ms. Fredrickson, would you sign my book? It is your most recent one."

Rance did the same thing with the book that he held as Little stepped back. The pair had heard that Dee and her friends were in the bookstore. It was a small town and the waitress liked to talk on the phone.

Dee laughed. "I, we, would be most happy to do so, gentlemen."

The book store owner stared at her. No one ever dared to call Rance and Little Fred gentlemen, not to their faces. Then she remembered that Dee had said the same thing to them the last time she had visited. It was something to wonder about.

Dee and Sandrel signed the books. "So, may we buy both of you a beer or two or three?" asked Dee.

Rance held out his arm. She slipped her arm around his. It was a very large arm.

"Come into my parlor," laughed Rance, "and we will just do that. We still have a special table in there. And it is still named, The Author's Corner." He laughed, a booming laugh that rattled the small window of the bookstore. He didn't tell her that no one would dare try to change it or take over that table for any other purpose. "Come on, Little. Let's go drink a bunch of beer. And show off our favorite author. I think there are probably a few other fans waiting, wanting their books signed as well. The young lady can have root beer. I don't think that Dee will hit us with that thing that she is carrying."

His happy laughter rattled the small window again. He thought that it was going to be a nice surprise for the bar patrons.

General Information

House Darthar.

Jonathon - Othara a'Anathor a'Mdator a'Zgura a'Winfa a'Relda d'Darthar - Head of House Darthar, and Lord of the Darthar family, both branches (Darthar and Darthar Na).

Karanly - Karanalador, first sister. She is the Damadon (sort of an Aunt) to Dee's daughters.

Jant - second brother - cross-tie to Nerela, Head, House Tartarnon.

Silneana - second sister.

Hakar - third brother - aiding Doma Sparta.

Aberly - third sister.

Rinil - fourth brother.

Antel - fourth sister.

House Darthar Na.

Dee - Daliera Fontala a'Anathor a'Mdator a'Zgura a'Winfa a'Relda d'Darthar Na. Head of House Darthar Na.

Ar - Ar'ga'da'fazza'din'ban'ahm'na. Dee's Advisor and Teacher.

Tiela - first daughter

Winala - second daughter, The Anointed One.

Doma Sparta - The People Historian, aided by Hakar of House Darthar, writing the history of The Feyra from their oral histories.

Groups resident in House Darthar Na.

The Seven Stands of The Fontala.

The Shadow Feyra - Cluster Head Moonat.

The House Beasts of Darthar Na.

Kartar - a great grizzly bear looking animal with thick, light green scales. One of them was named Gooda by Dee when she was a very young child.

The Inferno Hounds - horse sized animals that vaguely look like dogs. The four that are permanent residents of House Darthar Na, Dee named Manny, Moe, Jack, and Peter.

Furleen - lion sized, cougar looking, feline creatures with bronze colored fur and white tiger stripes on their shoulders and neck. Dee named the one of the house, Purr Cat.

Tarken - giant eagle-like birds who stand taller than most men, the pair are called Hack and Jack by Dee.

Hamel - also called Ice Cats - one was gifted to each of Daliera's daughters.

Sub-Houses of the Darthar.

suta Namel
suta Ean
suta Zbtan
suta Dundar
suta Milaton
    - who gifted the *Hamel,* the Ice Cats.
suta Ocedaron
suta Farbin

Dee's Cousin-Houses and their Heads.
> Dalir - Parlente
> Namata - Fam
> Induna - Armilin, Anointed One.
> Patal - Patal -a deeply hidden House, they gave the
> > Word's Ring back to Dee.
> Angorson - Pardosh
> Anathor - Fraz

House Sextet - The People group, "The "Council," an Adopted House of House Darthar Na.
> Head - Ralph Fredrickson & wife Sandra
> > Sandrel - their adopted daughter, a Feyra.
> Charles and Prentice James
> > Richlin - their daughter
> Randy and Anabelle Anders
> > Samuel and Samantha - their twins
> Daniel Fanzle - adopted into the house following The
> > Feyra practice, as suggested to Ralph by Dee.

House Hinterane - The Wild Garden
> Helsing - House Head
> Janice - Third Daughter.

The Fontala - Organization.

Daliera Fontala - The Word of The Fontala

Armilin ♀ - The One of The All - House Induna.

First Stand.

Amadur ♂ - First Hand - House Argonar.

Farlon ♂ - The One Who Remembers - House Faradon.

Second Stand

Meludo ♀ - First Hand - House Telat.

Delat ♀ - The One Who Remembers - House Trillmar.

Third Stand

Cantala ♀ - First Hand - House Zbtan.

Trakatar ♂ - The One Who Remembers - House Nerian.

Fourth Stand

Stregt ♂ - First Hand - House Ovever.

Wisuot ♀ - The One Who Remembers - House Zilan.

Fifth Stand

Mensta ♀ - First Hand - House Darunat.

Udoat ♀ - The One Who Remembers - House Hantaz.

Sixth Stand

Oatut ♀ - First Hand - House Quartep-Vierda.

Uztal ♂ - The One Who Remembers - House Abalam.

Seventh Stand

Kitea ♀ - First Hand - House Induna

Anagon ♀ - The One Who Remembers - House Naztan.

Yallan ♂ - The Seeker - House Farback.

♂ = male.

♀ = female.

About the Author

George R. Mead began to study anthropology in 1962 after being discharged (honorably) from the U. S. Army, Combat Engineers. He eventually received his degrees, a B.A., a M. A., and a Ph. D. in his chosen field. And many years later an M. S. W. in Clinical Social Work. He has worked in aerospace, taught at the college and university levels, worked in a community action agency, ran a restaurant, been unemployed, and worked for the U. S. Forest Service. He is now retired from the work-a-day world but does a certain amount of consulting, writing, and research. He lives seven miles outside of the small town of La Grande, Oregon, with his wife, two cats, and one dog. Rez joined the house as an eight-week old puppy found by Katy, a German Shepard (now deceased) under some brush in the middle of the American Southwest desert. Rez is now weighs 90 pounds down from 102 pounds (some puppy).